The Acorn Plan

The
Acorn Plan

TIM McLAURIN

W·W·Norton & Company

NEW YORK   LONDON

Printed in the United States of America.
The text of this book is composed in 12/13½ Bembo,
with display type set in Cloister Open Face.
Composition and manufacturing by
The Haddon Craftsmen, Inc.
Book design by Margaret M. Wagner

First published as a Norton paperback 1989

Library of Congress Cataloging-in-Publication Data
McLaurin, Tim.
The acorn plan / Tim McLaurin.
p. cm.
I. Title.
PS3563.C3843A64 1988
813'.54—dc19 87 32169

ISBN 0-393-30616-X

W. W. Norton & Company, Inc.
500 Fifth Avenue, New York, N.Y. 10110
W. W. Norton & Company Ltd.
10 Coptic Street, London WC1A 1PU

3 4 5 6 7 8 9 0

The Acorn Plan

1

BUBBLE RILEY decided to drink all the wine in the world the night Billy cut the soldier's lung in half. He made the pledge right after the Fayetteville police had gone, standing alone in front of Jerry's Burger Barn, staring at the puddle of blood and wishing they hadn't gotten so drunk.

Most of the crowd had left; seeing someone cut was not unusual at Jerry's, especially when Billy was around. They'd gone back to their cars, to their hot beer, cold hamburgers and nooky. But Bubble stood motionless for several minutes, his head lowered, mumbling, noticing how the soldier's blood was already congealing around the edges and how, against the black asphalt, it looked so very red.

Bubble walked to the curb and sat. Slowly he rocked, cradling his gut, which burned from all the wine. "Goddamn dumb-ass boy," he mumbled, shaking his head. He knew Billy hadn't set out to cut the soldier. They hadn't even planned on coming to Jerry's, but had considered going to the river and fishing for bullheads.

"Naw, not that, Bubble," Billy had said. "Last time you got so drunk I had to tote you back up the bank."

"You got a better idea?"

Billy took another swig of wine from the bottle they shared. "We could go over to Marge Thompson's house. I saw her today, and she said to stop by."

"She ain't wanting to see the two of us, old fart I am."

"Margie? Shit. She'd want the four of us if we were that many."

"Thought you said she's a claptrap."

Billy nodded while taking another guzzle of wine. "What about some pool? We could go over to Earl's Place and take them schoolboy's quarters."

"You forgetting you still owe Earl for that busted window?"

Bubble took the bottle from his nephew. He knew Billy was getting drunk. He was a damn good boy when sober, but lately Billy got a mean streak in him when he drank too much. That bothered Bubble.

"I wish your car was running," Billy said. "We could buy a case of beer and go to the drive-in flick."

Bubble nodded his head and felt sad. Just this week he had sold the battery. "What about the walk-in?"

"Naw, I don't like sitting in them nasty seats."

Bubble measured the bottle against the street light. Half empty. He felt even sadder.

"What say I run over to the grill and get another?" Billy asked.

"You don't need no more wine."

Billy laughed. "Man that's twenty-one don't have to drink milk." He scooted across the street and returned with another quart bottle. They sat on the up-turned Pepsi crates for half an hour more, passing the bottle and debating.

"We could go to the bowling alley on Raeford Road."

"Naw. The bus line is fixing to shut down."

"You hungry?" Billy asked.

"Yeah, come to think of it," Bubble answered. He tried to drink on an empty stomach. That way, the wine went further. Bubble emptied the bottle. It amazed him how quick bottles seemed to go these days.

Both were close to knee-walking when they left, so they weaved a course through backyards and alleys to keep out of sight of the cops. They reached the white cinder block, neon-lit diner, just as the car-privileged crowd was returning from downtown, mostly local people who leaned on their horns while backing into parking spaces. The people shouted to one another, drinking beer and tossing empty cans on the pavement.

More than a few lowered their voices when Billy stumbled by. Some even shut up altogether and sat quietly in their cars, a sensible practice when Billy was noticeably drunk.

Billy stepped onto a picnic table bench. "Sons of bitches," he roared. "Daughters of queers, Billy boy is here."

"Hush that kind of talk," Bubble grumbled.

"Why?"

"Cause the law will think you're drunk."

"I am drunk." Billy stepped on top of the concrete table. "Sons of sluts. Come here to Billy, and he'll slice your butts."

Billy jerked back his head and laughed, but no one in the cars did. They looked at their food. Bubble frowned until Billy stepped down, then went to the window and ordered a couple of hamburgers with fries.

"You sit down and eat this and sober up some," Bubble ordered.

Billy squeezed catsup on his fries, joked with Bubble, and watched cars circle the diner. He shouted at people he knew and at some he didn't know. Trouble rode in on the loud-motored '57 Chevy, candy-apple red, jacked high in the rear and sporting polished Crager mags. Billy watched it pass. The cam went whump, whump, whump and the stereo was cranked up loud.

"Bad ride, ain't it," Billy said.

The driver backed into a space, the engine revved several times, then shut down. The stereo kept blasting. A tall man with a soldier's short hair and bearing stepped out. He wore tight jeans and a T-shirt that revealed the legs of a nude lady tatooed on his right bicep. He bopped along to the diner, snapping his fingers to the music.

"Hey, buddy," Billy shouted. "What you pay for that rod?"

The soldier stopped and turned toward Billy. He peered over the rim of his shades, then walked on.

Billy squinted one eye at Bubble. He shouted louder. "I said there, my man, what you pay for that thing?"

"More money than you'll ever have," the soldier called over his shoulder. Then he leaned into the order window.

Billy tried to stand, but Bubble grabbed his arm. "Let it be," he warned.

"Hey, fuck you, grunt," Billy shouted at the soldier.

The soldier finished his order before he came over. "You got a problem, man?" He cocked one hand over his back pocket.

"Naw, not me," Billy said, carefully inspecting his fingernails. "Why you ask? You looking for a problem?"

"No. I just thought maybe you had a problem, that's all." The soldier turned to go.

"Hey, you with the airborne?" Billy asked.

"What if I am?"

"Cause I think the airborne sucks."

The soldier whirled back. Clutched in one fist gleamed the hooked blade of a paratrooper's knife. "Hey, fucker. I came here minding my own business. Might be best for you to do the same."

A crowd was quickly gathering in a semicircle, some grinning, but most watching with nervous eyes.

Slowly, Bubble stood. "Look, friend," he started.

"I ain't your friend, motherfucker."

"Well then, look here, mister. I'm sorry 'bout my nephew here. He's just real drunk. Why don't you go ahead and enjoy your food. We're real sorry."

The soldier hesitated before lowering the hand that held the knife. He tapped the side of the blade against his thigh. "O.K. Ain't no problem, pop. Just tell your boy to shut up his foul mouth."

"I'll do that. I sure will." Bubble turned and shook Billy's shoulder. "You stop it now, hear me?"

Billy leaned back on the bench against the table. His hands were behind his back. The soldier gave him a long, hard stare over his shades, then wheeled smartly about-face. "Dumb-ass hick," he said loudly.

"You suck. Airborne sucks. Your mama sucks," Billy taunted.

The soldier spun around on one heel and sliced in a wide arc. Billy came off the bench smooth and quick, slipping underneath the blade, and slashed across with his hawk-billed blade, catching the soldier under his armpit between two ribs. The sound was easy, just the rip of cloth, but the blade didn't surface until it reached the sternum and brought out chunks of pink lung. The soldier looked very surprised. He dropped his blade and knelt slowly, holding his ribs and moaning. Blood flowed from between his fingers, ran down his shirt and dripped on the pavement. He was still kneeling when the ambulance arrived.

2

BILLY knew there was no sense in running. Too many people there knew him, and besides, he felt a curious interest in the way the man knelt, his face white and his palm jammed tight against his chest. Somehow he seemed much more human now than when he was a bopping, juke-walking bad ass.

Billy slipped the knife to Bubble, then sat down on the curb and waited for the police to come screeching up.

The officers didn't rough him any; all the ones who worked the east side of Fayetteville had known Billy's father. They just snapped on a set of handcuffs and drove him to Central Station. He was locked in a cell along with several drunks, where he bent forward on a cot and drummed his fingers against the side of his head. An hour later, he was led into a small office for questioning.

"Why'd you cut him?" asked the detective.

Billy shrugged. "I don't know. I guess I was trying to save his life."

"Don't be a wise ass with me, Billy. I've known you since you were knee-high."

Billy shrugged again. He was led back to the cell.

Billy knew that Bubble had already made the call, and that Wallace Bain would be down in the morning to pay his bail, so he stretched out on the filthy bunk, watched the drunks cry and cuss, and chewed on his fingernails. Later, he slept the dreamless, snoring sleep that comes from too much wine.

It seemed Billy had just closed his eyes when he awakened to naked, electric lights, his tongue thick and temples throbbing. Someone was calling his name. He sat up and before him stood the jailer with Wallace Bain, stiff and out of place in his gray linen suit. Wallace wasn't frowning, but his eyes said he was fed up and worried. He stood over Billy's cot for several seconds. Then he did frown, so Billy frowned back and wished his head didn't hurt.

"He'll be all right," Billy said. "Lung meat always heals fast."

Wallace exhaled heavily. "Maybe, maybe not. We don't know for sure yet. One thing I do know, is that you're not all right."

"Yeah? As in why?"

"Jesus Christ, Billy! Three times in four months." Wallace lowered his voice. "The prosecutor says he's going to ask for attempted murder."

"Bull. For cutting someone? Hey, he swung first." Billy swallowed, the sound of it loud in his own ears. "If I'd wanted to kill him, I'd gone for his neck."

Wallace shook his head deliberately and stared at the concrete floor. The drunks watched Billy with new respect. "I can't figure you out anymore," Wallace said. "Just can't." He walked to the bars, then spun back. "I'm just glad your dad doesn't have to see this. It would kill Mike deader than that heart attack."

"Oh, he probably sees all right," Billy answered, narrowing his eyes. "Ain't you supposed to be able to see everything from up there?"

"For God's sake, Billy. You're nearly twenty-two. A grown man. What the hell is going on?" Wallace pulled out a handkerchief from his back pocket and mopped his forehead. "You know," he said quietly, "you might get time for this. Six months is a real possibility."

"Just get my bail, how 'bout? You're a lawyer, remember? Not a preacher."

"Yeah, well maybe I ain't no preacher, but I was your dad's

best friend. And I've known you since you were shitting yellow."

"Just get my bail, O.K.?"

"If I was about five years younger right now, I'd bust your ass good."

Wallace's face colored deep red and a thick vein stood out on his forehead. Then Billy smiled, the smile that could take anyone, his face lighting up and his eyes sparkling like troubled water. "Hey, you're sounding like you're back on the corner with my old man."

Wallace smacked fist into palm. He sighed. "I wish to hell you had another couple of years in the Marines. You still don't have any discipline."

"Get me out of here, Wallace," Billy repeated, the smile erased from his face. "I don't like it in here."

"It's going to take some time. I've got some convincing to do."

"I swear. I'll go straight as a hoe handle."

"The judge said no bail until they know this guy is going to be O.K."

"He'll make it. I wasn't cutting to kill."

Wallace left then, but didn't return for five days.

3

ON Monday morning Bubble walked out on his job. He marched into the boss's office and put it right on the line.

"I'm quitting, Harry. As of this very minute," he said to the pot-bellied, balding man behind the wide, metal desk. "Just give me my time and what other, and I'll be gone."

The boss rubbed his fleshy chin. He sat forward. "Quit? Why do you want to quit?"

"Personal reasons, sick of this place, running for mayor. Take your pick."

"My God, Bubble. You better give this some thought."

"I've thought."

The boss stood, then walked to the window overlooking the guts of the mill. Over his shoulder, Bubble saw bodies scurrying between the huge, whining machines. He turned and looked Bubble in his eyes. "What do you think Mike would have said about this?"

Bubble's top lip curled slightly. Twenty years he had been in the plant, but had never been promoted above general floor help because of his week-long drunks. "Mike can't say nothing now. Jobs don't matter much to dead men."

So Bubble left the drab interior of the cotton mill for the last time, punched the clock and heard it snap neatly through the paper card, and strode out through the shadows of the twin smokestacks. He was given three day's back wages, a week's vacation pay, and the cashed-in value of his insurance plan—a little more than six hundred dollars all totaled. He hid most of it in a sock in a hole in the bottom of his mattress. Then he headed downtown with two tens in his pocket.

Ordinarily, the squat, sad houses of east Fayetteville would have held nothing new for Bubble. Years back, he had ceased to mark how every day the buildings settled closer to the dirt and concrete, turned grayer like mushrooms that have passed their prime. The community was just home to him and all the others at the mill, to the truckers and plumbers and waitresses and route salesmen. But today, he did notice, now a liberated man, shocked at how the houses were rickety as wet cardboard, the brief spots of color from flowers planted inside discarded tires, and candy-striped, rusty swingsets, only highlighting the decay. Billy was decaying too. Bubble picked up his gait at the thought as he hurried to Willie's Bar and Grill. He took the shortcut that skirted the river through the back lot where the winos hung out.

"Hey, Bubble," a drunk shouted from the shade of a tree. "What brings you here on a Monday?"

"Got business with Willie," Bubble answered.

The winos exchanged glances. Six of them rested in various stages of drunk, but even the drunkest managed to prop himself up on one elbow. Bubble was good drinking company because he was generous and hated to be alone.

"Kind'a early for ya, ain't it?" asked Shorty Bullard, a stocky, red-faced man with bad teeth.

"Don't matter none," Bubble said. "I've turned over a new leaf." Deep down, Bubble realized he was an alcoholic, and had been for years. So far he had managed to keep his drinking within reason, limiting it to weekends except for occasional binges. He wasn't in the same league as those who spent their days and nights behind Willie's bar, having kept up a house and held onto his job until now.

"A new leaf, huh?" Shorty's eyes widened. "You ain't giving up drinking?"

"No. Nothing like that. I'm aiming to drink more."

That jolted everyone. Several managed to sit up and rub their eyes. Shorty smiled.

"Well, I think I can speak for all of us in saying we'd be glad to have you join us if you're planning on pulling a drunk. We've got some sardines and crackers, and I've got a snort here to get you jump-started."

Shorty passed him a green bottle containing two fingers of wine. Bubble sniffed the top, then took a swallow. The wine was hot and acidic, but he swallowed quickly and wiped his mouth on his sleeve. Shorty took the bottle and drained the last drop. Bubble stood in silence, gazing at the failed men.

"I need some professional advice from you fellows," he said finally.

Shorty nodded, then looked at the other winos who nodded as well. "Well, there ain't no PhD in the whole lot here, but we'll give you our best."

"I need to know this. What is the worst wine in the world for making a fellow crazy? You know, shooting and cutting crazy."

"That's a tough one. Why d'ya want to know?"

"Cause I aim to drink all of it."

"All of it?"

"Yeah, if it's in me, I aim to drink all the wine in the world."

The winos stared blankly at Bubble, wondering if they had heard him right. Then Shorty chuckled and the others joined him in a chorus of laughter.

"Can't nobody drink all the wine in the world, Bubble," Shorty said. "Hell, I been trying all my life and ain't made a dent."

Their laughter galled him, but Bubble faked a chuckle of his own.

"I mean it," Bubble said. "I want to know what is the worst wine in the world. Crazy-making wine."

The winos put their heads together and discussed the matter intensely, each one arguing for his favorite brand.

"You want to get crazy, you ought to drink 'bout a fifth of Richard's Triple Peach," said Chubby Watts. "That shit'll make you run rabbits."

"Bullshit," said Larry Cooper, his brimmed fishing hat pulled even with his eyebrows to hide a recently stitched-up forehead. "Richard's wouldn't make my dick hard. You want to raise hell, drink you a gut full of Thunderbird."

Punk Davis spit in the dirt. "Shit, Larry. All Thunderbird did for you was get your ass whupped. Ask me, Roma Rocket is best. Don't make you sleepy, either."

"Ain't nobody asked you," Larry answered, and pulled his cap a little lower.

Shorty held his arm and shouted for silence. "Quit the arguing. Hell, we'll ask Clarence. He's the authority on hell raising."

Shorty walked to where Clarence Hubbard lay passed out in the edge of some bushes. He shook him several times and slapped his face. Clarence moaned, then spoke several unintelligible words. Shorty felt under the man's belly and pulled out a nearly empty bottle of wine. He held it away from his face and read the label.

"M.D. 20/20. 'da Mad Dog. If Clarence drinks it, it's gotta be bad," he said, handing the bottle to Bubble.

"Yeah, Clarence would know," said Chubby, a half-burned cigarette jiggling between his lips as he talked. "He's cut a lot of people."

"Shot a nigger once, too," another said.

Bubble nodded. He crunched on a saltine cracker. Then he marched into Willie's and bought a case of Mad Dog.

THE early fall weather was good, clear days without rain and nights warm enough to prevent much dew. Bubble lounged with his new friends, drinking much wine, dining off sardines and potted meat and crackers and liver pudding. He drank under the shade of a willow tree and slept there, cushioned with a long piece of cardboard and musty pillow, only returning home to take more money from the hole under his mattress. He tried to forget that Billy was three days now in jail, but still called Wallace, the family lawyer, regular to see if bond had been set.

Bubble stuck to drinking Mad Dog, and for a while he thought it might actually be possible to drink all the crazy-making wine in the world, or at least all in Willie's Bar and Grill. Anyway, his real objective was to show Billy just how disgusting and wasted alcohol could make a man. Bubble realized he hadn't cared about his own life for years now, but he cared about the boy, and he'd show him. He'd show him goddamn well what wine would do to you. That afternoon a delivery truck arrived and loaded Willie's shelves with wine again, and Bubble realized what a task he had. He set to with renewed vigor, and soon word spread to every drunk east of the river that a real party was going on.

Bubble had always likened the drunks behind Willie's to autumn leaves a cold rain has plastered against sidewalks and car tops, their colors muted and leeched. They wore mismatched and ill-sized clothes snatched from backyard lines and Salvation Army bins: checkered trousers paired with striped shirts, old coats with busted sleeves, one wing-tip loafer teamed with a tennis shoe laced up with fishing line. Their teeth were bad, the men's chins unshaven, skinned elbows and infected insect bites slow to heal, then leaving white scars. Their eyes were dimmed by wine and the personal griefs they chose years before to never see again. Yep, like old leaves, fading fast but slowly dying.

Among the dying were Chubby Watts, so skinny he tied his trousers with a length of rope, and Punk Davis, and Wilma, Punk's old lady, who would screw anyone for a bottle, and Shorty, who was short, and Milton and Larry Cooper, who had once run a fish market before they began drinking up the rent, and Clarence, who was half Cherokee Indian and half crazy and had killed a nigger once, and Mary the Queen, a fat woman from somewhere up north who sold queenly blow jobs, and Harry Little, who had lost a leg in Viet Nam and would cry "In coming! In coming!" when he was very drunk. They clustered within the shade of the tree with about a dozen others who drifted in and out, and drank and ate and slept and puked and fucked and coughed there, and shit in the blueberry bushes growing on the banks of Cape Fear. Sometimes they fell backwards from their squat and rolled into the deep, gray water and drowned. They were all bums, had been, would be.

But not Bubble. He knew he wasn't a bum, just a man with a weakness for drink, prone to fall hard occasionally for a few days, only to get sick and spit up blood and be cared for by his sister Ruby until he could return to work. But this time was different. He wasn't drinking from weakness, he was drinking with conviction.

Ruby came on the morning of the fourth day. She was wearing her starched, white waitress uniform, her red hair piled high in its usual coil, her meaty arms folded over her bosom while she frowned.

"What in hell do you think you're doing?" She towered above where Bubble sat; her words had the ring of one scolding a child.

Bubble cocked an eye from where he was eating a can of cold pork and beans. He took a moment to focus his vision. "Hey there, little sister."

Ruby grunted. "Couldn't you have at least let someone know where you were?"

"I know where I am," Bubble finally answered. He spit a bean into the grass. "So does the gang here."

Ruby squinted a mean eye at the bums under the tree. She wrinkled her nose. "I meant human beings. Not a bunch of hogs."

"They ain't hogs. They're my buddies."

"Yeah," Chubby answered. "We're his friends."

Ruby stared at the red creases across Chubby's thin face from sleeping squashed against the ground. His fly was open, his shirttail pulled through the hole.

"I take it back. I don't mean hogs. Hog shit is a better description."

"Somebody should slap her face," said Wilma. "Who is she to be so high and mighty?"

"Watch your mouth," Bubble warned. "This here's my sister."

Ruby stared at the small woman till Wilma dropped her eyes to the ground, then turned her anger back to Bubble. "I'm ashamed to claim you right now. I hear you even quit your job."

"Wasn't much of one."

"It kept you living, didn't it?"

"No." Bubble took another swig from his bottle. "Actually, I think it kept me dying."

Ruby watched a trickle of wine leak from the corner of Bubble's mouth and drip from his jaw to the front of his shirt. His shoes were off, one big toe poking through a hole in his sock.

"I suppose you think all this wine you're drinking is gonna do you good?"

"Damn right," said Milton Cooper. "See the bloom in his cheeks?"

"Yeah, I see it, hog shit, bloom in his cheeks with bloodshot eyes, stinking, sitting there eating cold pork and beans. I see it."

"You're looking at it all wrong, Ruby," Shorty said. "Bubble ain't killing himself, he's healing himself. Timothy 5:23, and I quote Saint Paul, 'Drink no longer water, but use a little wine for thy stomach's sake and thine often infirmities.'"

"He didn't mean lay around drinking rot gut."

"If you don't like it, hit the road, honey," said Mary the Queen, crossing her arms and cocking her head to one side. A grimy crease between her double chins made her throat look slit.

"I said for ya'll to shut up," Bubble hollered. "I can handle my own sister."

"Make me leave, whore," Ruby said to Mary. Ruby stood at five-foot-ten and weighed 170 pounds, with thick calloused hands that were capable of pulling out gobs of hair. Mary snorted, then spit on the ground, but shut up.

"You even been to see Billy yet?" Ruby asked.

"No," Bubble mumbled, then ducked his eyes. "I been in touch with Wallace, though, and he's taking care of everything."

"Well, he's got his work cut out for him this time. That soldier nearly bled to death."

Several bums moved away from the argument to sleep. Bubble fiddled with a loose button on his shirt.

"I talked to Harry today, and he said to tell you that if you'll be at work tomorrow, he'll give you one last chance."

"I can't do that," Bubble said while slowly shaking his head. "I got to do this thing for Billy."

"For Billy?" Ruby cried, her eyes wide. "For Billy?"

"Yeah, for Billy."

"How do you figure laying up drunk and losing your job is gonna help Billy?"

"That boy has got to see right damn soon what drinking will do to ya." Bubble raised his chin. "I plan to drink every drop in the world."

The few drunks still conscious grinned.

"All the wine in the world, huh? You're a fool." Ruby turned and started for her car. "A damn fool." She shouted this over and over before reaching her battered green Plymouth and driving away.

BUBBLE and his followers slept through the hot afternoon, awakening at twilight with rat nests and cobwebs filling their heads and mouths. They pooled their money, Bubble providing most of it, and purchased another case of wine. An old tire was doused with kerosene and lit. They sat in the dancing light,

eating from cans and smoking, passing the bottles until drunkenness again swept over them like a soft, warm wave. One of the
bums had a coughing spell, and the sound of him starving for
breath reminded Bubble of how Mike had sounded in his last
few weeks.

"This is a free way to be, ain't it?" Bubble said to anyone
listening. "Being a bum is a free way for a man to live."

A pause. "Yeah," Chubby answered. "Free to work a little,
or never work, sleep when you feel like it, and drink when you
can. Hell, I could up and thumb down to Florida tomorrow."

"Free way to die, too, ain't it," Bubble continued, looking
into the fire. "Men let lots of things kill them, but usually they
suffer too long. Shit, a man could drink himself to death in six
months if he tried."

"Quicker than that," Chubby answered. "I knew a fellow who
had been drunk just five days when he passed out, puked and
croaked."

"After just five days?"

"Yep, young guy. Wasn't no bum, neither. Had just split up
from his wife. Went to sleep on his back and that was it."

"I don't wanna drown in wine puke."

"Me neither, but you got to admit, it's quicker than laying up
with your liver gone."

Bubble nodded. "Good to know there's a few things we can
control in this old world."

Soon most of the bums were sleeping, curled on their pads
like babies, what valuables or money they owned stuffed in their
crotches. Bubble sat alone by the fire, thinking drunk, jumbled
thoughts. For a second, he imagined he saw Mike's face in the
flames, not a bad face, but the way his older brother had looked
in his good days. The face disappeared with a twist of the flames
and Bubble shook his head.

"Strong-ass wine." He took another swig. "Crazy-making
wine." Bubble stood, rubbed his knees, then headed for his
cardboard pad beside the bushes, wavering with his feet striking

the ground heavily and flat. "Goddamn strong-ass wine," he mumbled again. He flopped down and began pulling at his shoes. He jumped when a second face appeared in the darkness.

"Damn, Wilma! Scare me to death." Bubble slapped at his chest and coughed.

"Sorry, Bubble. Just thought I would say goodnight."

"Yeah? That's nice of 'ya. Well, good night. Say, where's Punk?"

"Over there passed out."

Wilma was short and skinny with a sharp face and large front teeth like a rodent's. Her breasts were too large for her body. She was wearing a stained pair of white painter's pants and a ridiculous laced blouse that might have been part of some rich woman's evening suit. Her hair was mostly gray.

"Yeah? Well, sleep tight, hear," Bubble said. He continued taking off his shoes.

Wilma sat down heavily on the grass. She hugged her knees. "Punk was telling me you got a house?"

"Yeah. Sort of. I rent it."

"Then why you sleeping out here with these bums? Might rain even tonight."

"Houses don't mean nothing to me 'cept a place to sleep."

"Then sleep there."

Bubble wrenched off his second shoe. He picked at the goo between his toes. Wilma slid closer. She traced one finger across his arm.

"Bubble honey. You ought not to be sleeping outside like this. Gonna be cold soon. You'll get sick." She leaned a little closer, then smiled. "Say, what if I was to move in with you? I can cook real good, and clean up, and be good company at night."

"You already got Punk."

"The hell with Punk. He's always lying in his puke."

"The last thing I need right now is a woman."

"Why? You're a man." Wilma slid her finger down his arm across his leg, lightly drawing circles around his crotch. "Think about it, baby. We could have a real nice time together." The circles she drew pressed heavier and heavier until she was vigorously rubbing his penis.

"Oh God," Bubble whispered, feeling the heat gather. Wilma took his hand and placed it between her thighs. "Oh shit," he said.

Wilma slid off her pants in seconds, then helped Bubble off with his, and pulled him on top of her upon the cardboard bed.

"You might have a point," Bubble said. "It's been awhile."

They had barely begun to grind together when Bubble felt hot stinging on his rear end. "Goddamn it," he yelped and jumped to his knees, turning to see Punk waving the neck of a shattered wine bottle in small circles.

"I got something right here you can fuck," Punk growled.

Bubble felt his buttocks with one hand, the other stretched up before him. "Goddamn. Hold on now, Punk," he said backing up. "I was just leaving."

Bubble took off running, his pants down around his ankles, arms pumping, leaving the good life behind him in back of Willie's Bar and Grill.

"GODDAMN IT, blow, blow," Bubble hollered later that night while Ruby cleaned his wounds with alcohol. He craned his head back from where he lay on her green vinyl couch, trying to watch what she was doing, his butt bare and streaked with two long, red wounds. Ruby swabbed the cuts and swore right back at him.

"I hope it burns. Laying around like some cur dog. How the hell did you do this, anyway? Must've had your pants off. Ain't no cuts in your pants."

"I was shitting and fell back on a busted bottle."

"I really believe that one."

"You believe what you want. Just get me fixed up."

"You ought to have stitches. A couple of places look bad."

"Naw, they don't. Just stick on some Band-Aids and let it go."

"Stupid drunk. Stupid asshole drunk."

Bubble fell asleep that night on his belly in Ruby's living room. The next morning there was fire across his backside, but after soaking in a bathtub of hot water and epsom salts, he felt better and was capable of walking, though stiffly. Ruby fed him eggs and fatback, grits and coffee, lectured him, then pitied him, and finally left for the diner after making him swear to stay put.

Bubble thought about staying for a while as he sopped up the last of the egg yolk, even considered hobbling back down to the mill to ask Harry for that job. Then he remembered the animal looking out of Billy's eyes the night he slit the soldier. He laid down the scrap of toast and went out to buy another jug of wine.

4

THE days passed slowly in the pokey. Billy played cards with the other brawlers who rotated in and out daily, read two cheap western novels he borrowed from the jail chaplain and masturbated once when the cell was dark and everyone was snoring. He ate his meals slowly, grinding the tough stew beef and canned green beans into a pulp, and watched the door to the cell block for Wallace's return. He did this for nearly a week.

"I was beginning to think you had forgotten me," he said with a tenuous grin when Wallace finally arrived. "I was beginning to think I was going to have to try some of that Papillon stuff."

"Well, don't think I've been duck hunting all week. I had to call up every favor that was owed me in the county to get you out. You're damn lucky that soldier survived."

"I told you he would," said Billy.

The jailor unlocked the door and handed Billy a brown paper sack containing his wallet, sneaker laces, belt and fifty-seven cents in change. Then he signed over several papers swearing to appear in court in two weeks, and was free to go. The sunshine made him shield his eyes as he walked to Wallace's car.

"So what'd you get the charges dropped to?" Billy asked as they drove out of the parking lot.

"Simple assault. It's all a formality now. The judge will sentence you to one year in prison, suspend it, and place you on probation for three years."

"Probation? That'll mean I can't leave the state."

"He's also going to appoint me as your probation officer."

"That's better."

"But you fuck up once more, even a fist fight, and your ass goes up river."

"Like I told you. Straight as a hoe handle," Billy said, squinting his eyes as he gazed out the car window. He rubbed his chin. "Say, how's that soldier?"

"He's all right. It's a good thing you're a southpaw."

"I hate that I cut him now. Almost wish I could tell him so."

"Then why did you?"

"I don't know. He started it. Maybe I'm a little bit crazy."

"You can't get away with that excuse."

"Sometimes I feel like I'm going to smother."

Wallace downshifted the car while turning into McDonald's. "Just remember, Billy, once more, and Jesus won't be able to spring you."

The girl behind the service window smiled with all her teeth. She took their order, stuffed a paper sack full of burgers and fries, then dropped in extra packs of catsup.

"Enjoy your meal and thank you for stopping," she said, eyeing Billy and his week-old beard.

"Nice tits, huh?" Billy said.

"I wasn't looking."

"You ain't been locked up for a week, either."

They drove through the Haymont section on the west side of Fayetteville—the good part of town that saddled the high ground above the river—then turned onto Hay Street toward the old span bridge that dropped to the flats of the east.

"There were a couple of conditions I had to consent to for your release," Wallace said. The bridge greeted them as always in red spray paint, "Jenny Wilson Fucks."

"Yeah?" Billy cocked his head. "What?"

"You have to go to work and stop hanging around the streets, and you have to visit a therapist at least three times."

"Where am I going to get a job?"

"I've already taken care of that."

"I'm not going to any shrink."

"It's that or go to jail."

At the first stoplight beyond the bridge, Billy asked to be let out, shook Wallace's hand, then took the shortcut to Bubble's house beside the river, past the winos guzzling their rot-gut wine. Billy found him sleeping in a rocking chair on his front porch, his head flopped backwards, a dribble of saliva leaking from the corner of his mouth. Crammed between his knees was an empty wine bottle.

Bubble had resumed drinking with gusto after leaving Ruby's house, partly from his commitment to Billy, and partly to ease the pain of healing cuts.

"Medicine," he called after downing the first bottle. "Medicine to ease an aching ass and an aching world."

Billy watched the way his uncle's chest rose and fell, the way his eyelids fluttered as if watching something in a dream. Then he picked up a straw from the floor and stuck one end up Bubble's nose.

"What the goddamn," Bubble sputtered, slapping at his face. He opened his eyes, smiled, then sat forward, wiping the trickle of spit from his cheek. "Shit, boy, thought you were a bug."

"Thought you were a turd, the way you're just laying there. You're starting to smell like one." Billy slapped the older man on the shoulder. "How you doing, anyway?"

"Not too bad. Can't complain. Pulling one hell of a drunk. Hey, you're the one that's been locked up. I was beginning to think they had ya."

"Naw, just had to wait for Wallace to play his games."

Bubble lifted the bottle and frowned when he found it empty. He set it on the floor. Billy watched how slowly he moved, his eyes bloodshot, his clothes stained with old sweat.

"Yeah, I heard you were pulling a big one."

"That right? Who told you such a thing?"

"I just heard it. You know how word gets around."

"Well, it ain't none of their business. Man of fifty-one ought to be able to take a snort when he damn well pleases."

"I hear you quit your job, too."

Bubble grimaced as he squirmed higher in his chair, then reached to rub his lower back. "Wasn't quitting much 'cept pushing a broom."

"How you plan on eating?"

"I'm giving up food. It never gave me nothing but a big belly and brown shit. I'm just drinking from now on."

"Then I'll drink with you. You have another jug?"

"No, not for you I don't. You get crazy when you drink. I'm gonna drink all the wine in the world."

"That's impossible."

"Yeah, well I've made a pretty good start on it already."

"I can see that," Billy said, the smile leaving his face. "You're going to kill yourself, too."

"Yeah, well maybe," Bubble said, looking Billy in his eyes. "But it's better an old shit like me die than you keep on drinking and fighting till you ruin your life."

Billy narrowed his eyes and studied Bubble. "So, you're saying that you're gonna be a bad example to me, and show me the wages of sin?"

"Damn right."

"That's crazy talk, and I ain't listening to it. I ain't to blame for your drinking." Billy walked off the porch and hopped the low wire fence.

"What's the matter?" Bubble called after him. "You got to be drinking to make conversation?"

"If I was drunk, what you're saying might make more sense," Billy answered.

BILLY walked fast for the first block, then slowed and scanned both sides of the street. Nothing had changed in a week.

Damn ugly place, Billy thought. Still, it's better than jail. The dusty windows of the houses seemed to stare at him like

blind eyes. Brown and gray houses that had once been white, blue or yellow when men with dreams as bright as the paint built them. But, dreams couldn't survive in them long; the outside, weathered and faded and sagging, showed what the lives inside had become.

Billy began to whistle, trying to drown out the story the houses seemed to be whispering as well as Bubble's crazy talk.

Ain't no such thing as dreams coming true, Billy. Might as well forget that, boy, and go on down to that sprawling mill and punch in and watch the swirling belts and bobs till your head spins too, and take it till the horn blows and you can say the hell with it all and leave with your lunch pail in one hand and your coat slung over your shoulder, and head for one of the bars where you can slug down beer after beer till most of your senses are numb before going home to face that wife who was once so pretty, and lift those younguns who kiss and cling and smell of sour milk and shit.

Billy picked up the tune he whistled and set his feet down hard, ignoring the cry of the houses, peeling paint and rotting boards, the paths beaten from every door through the red, packed clay, paths by which men had left and returned and left, left, left. He passed cats taking a midafternoon nap, yapping dogs busy scavenging the garbage cans, and old people who rocked on their porches, watching the day slowly turn. A few waved when he walked by, but most just looked to that private spot that only they could see.

Billy refused to listen or notice today; he bopped along as if spring were in his legs. The afternoon seemed fine and blue following days without the sun. He sucked down the cool snap in the air and listened to the soft rustle of leaves overhead whisper that fall was coming. When he passed the old place, he gave it only a glance, the house that had stood out with clipped hedges and bright red shutters. It was dead now, too, along with Mike, the spirit leaving the walls as quickly as smoke on the wind.

Further down the road, Ruby was in her daffodil bed, the one that Billy had built from old crossties and a truckload of top soil. She worked on her knees, digging into the soft humus with a trowel, dropping bulbs into the furrows. She looked up at the squeal of the gate, her smile plumping her cheeks, causing wrinkles to fan out from her hazel eyes.

"Billy, honey," she sighed, and went to hug him, rounds of damp earth clinging to the skin on her knees. "Billy, Billy."

"Hey, Ruby," he smiled. "You sure like playing in the dirt."

She squeezed him, then, pulling his long body against the fullness of her breasts, and held him there as if there was a hunger inside her only he could feed.

"You O.K.?" she asked, pulling back to plant a wet kiss on his cheek. "You're all right, ain't you?"

" 'Course," he said, and grinned as he pinched her cheek. "It was like laying up in a hotel."

"I wanted to come and see you," she said, suddenly blinking rapidly while staring at the ground. "I wanted to so bad, but I just couldn't go in that place."

"Shoot. Don't worry about it." He squeezed her again. "I had new company every night."

"I know you're starving, you must be." Ruby took hold of his sleeve and led him through the front door. "I'm going to make you the best meal of your life."

"Just fix me a sandwich."

If the houses of east Fayetteville mirrored a generation's defeat, Ruby's place shouted that here was one soul who refused to give up. She had filled the corners and crannies of her yard with bright colored flowers and shrubs, she painted the fence yearly and displayed a gaudy, pink bird bath that attracted robins and blue jays. On the north side of the house where winter winds blistered the paint worst, she had planted ivy. Over the years, the ivy crept upwards till now it was a rich, green blanket that covered the wall, cheering even during February rains. She had scrubbed the inside floors with Pine-Sol and

water until the wood grain stood out as bold as in newly split lumber. Numerous vases of plastic flowers sat on shelves, K-Mart pictures of the Southwest, a crucifix over the door, though she wasn't Catholic, and vinyl covers on the table, sofa and chairs. It was the house of a woman who believed that in the end the good ones win out.

Will you win? A nagging, inner voice asked Ruby even as she opened the door to the refrigerator. Will it come? Will you win in the end?

She often awoke late at night, alone, with the memories of her three miscarried babies, alone, with horrors of the day she watched Larry laid to rest after a knife fight in the county jail.

Will it come to you, Ruby, the voice nagged as she reached for the can of lard, if you hurt enough, if you wait long enough, if you give enough?

Who will bring it to you? It seems impossible to do alone. Maybe one of the truckers, those lonely men who ride that ribbon of concrete over the horizen to the places you have longed to see. Maybe it is there, under the soft, warm belly of one special road cowboy, something lasting passing from his loins into yours. Maybe? All you can do is wait and hope, and with each failure place another vase of bright flowers upon the mantel, or dig into the earth until your fingers are torn and sore.

Splat, into the hot frying pan Ruby dropped a gob of lard and again she was too busy to worry.

Billy helped himself to a beer while Ruby scurried about, rattling pots and pans and placing potatoes on the table to peel. He drank the beer fast, then cracked another. Ruby frowned at the sound of hissing beer, but continued working with the machine-like precision of twenty-plus years in a truck-stop cafe, slicing and paring, filling the room with the crackle of hot grease and the good odor of meat frying.

"You want some biscuits? I know you can eat some biscuits."

"What you have there is fine. I've eaten already."

"You need some biscuits. It won't take me but a minute."

Ruby hurried, mixing flour and buttermilk, salt and lard, kneading and rolling the dough with her hands. She glanced at Billy. "You've lost some weight." When the dough no longer stuck to her fingers, she mashed out patties, dipped them in flour, placed them on a cookie sheet and stuck it in the oven. Then she opened herself a beer and sat on the couch beside him.

"You're not working today?" Billy asked.

"Tonight. I've got to work the night shift till some of this Labor Day freight slows down."

"You shouldn't have to work nights, as long as you've been there. It ain't safe."

"It'll be just a couple of weeks."

"Still ain't fair."

The pork chops sputtered and popped and filled the house with good smells. Ruby sipped her beer and stared at the floor, her brow worried.

"Why don't you go ahead and say it?" Billy asked. "Go ahead and ask me why I cut that guy."

She took a deep breath. "Well, why did 'ya, Billy?"

"What can I say? I don't know. The guy was acting like a jerk. I lost my head." Billy paused to take another swallow. "Maybe I was just born mean like the Tatums and Bains."

Ruby jerked her head up. "You can't use that excuse. There ain't a mean bone in you."

"Well, maybe I've grown to be that way."

"I don't believe it. I don't believe it for one minute."

Ruby quickly stood and went to turn the meat. "You're too good for this neighborhood," she called over her shoulder. "I want you to get out of here."

"Yeah? And where am I supposed to go?"

"School, like we talked about."

"What's college going to do for me? Bubble went for two years and look at him now. The hook's set deep, Ruby."

"Well, maybe you'll be the fish that gets away," Ruby said, turning to him with her hands on her hips. "You ever think of that? Maybe you'll be the first of the Rileys."

5

ON Monday morning, Billy got up at seven and hit the street to report for his first day of work at the pet shop. He paused at the middle of the bridge and looked at the river, the water low from two straight weeks without rain. A thin fog wafted over the surface, muting the splintered ends of a floating tree trunk. The channel was still in shadows, the water colored like pewter, a low sun glinting orange through the tree limbs. Occasionally, the surface erupted where brim fed on insects.

Wish I could get my cane pole and spend the day doing nothing but fishing and sipping beer, he lamented, instead of selling fucking cat litter.

Sadly, he turned away and was soon standing in front of the darkened pet shop, waiting for the owner and feeling a great deal of reluctance in his belly.

Through the glass, he could see the shapes and shadows of live creatures in tanks and cages, swimming and scurrying as they woke to the growing light. Billy pressed his face to the pane, and as his eyes became accustomed to the dim interior, spied a cage of fat white rats. They sat on their haunches, peering back at him through the wire.

Rats, Billy thought. I'm going to be selling rats.

The rodents twitched their noses and stood against the wire. A human shape meant food.

"Stop breathing on the glass," said a voice behind him. Billy, startled, bumped the window with his forehead.

"Now you've got it greasy," the voice spoke again.

Billy turned and faced a tall, barrel-chested man wearing

spectacles. A half-moon scar curved across one cheek. The man stared at Billy while fishing a ring of keys from his pocket.

"I take it you're the boy Wallace spoke to me about?"

"Well, if you're Mr. Banner, then I guess I'm your boy."

"At least you're on time."

After the man unlocked a dead bolt and swung open the door, Billy followed him inside. "Don't need any of that fancy electrical stuff," Banner said. "Just good strong wood and steel."

The shop smelled strongly of cedar chips, with a distinct back-up odor of urine. Billy wrinkled his nose. A dog yelped at their arrival, followed by the whistle of a scarlet macaw, the twittle of a pair of love birds. A Siamese kitten stood against its cage front and mewed.

"Quiet, quiet," Banner shushed, while flipping a switch. The neon bulbs flickered, warming, then sudden brightness filled the room. Banner glanced quickly around the pet shop, scanning the long rows of wire pens and fish tanks. Finally, he nodded his head, then motioned for Billy to follow him. They zig-zagged down the aisles to a small back office. Billy was told to sit in a straight-back armchair while Banner fumbled in his desk, thrusting an application under his face.

"Fill this out," he grunted.

Afterwards, Banner grunted some more while reading what Billy had written, looking up occasionally from the paper to Billy's face.

"Been in the military, huh?" he finally said, peering over the top of his glasses.

"Yes sir. Marines for three years."

"Why just three? I pulled twenty-two."

"Three years was a plenty for me. You served in the Marines?"

"Hell, no. The Army."

Billy drew small circles on his pants leg while Banner finished reading.

"What has three stripes up and two under," he barked suddenly.

"A gunny sergeant."

"What's a John Wayne?"

"A can opener."

"Who was Chesty Puller?"

"The best general that ever drew breath."

Banner paused and raised one eyebrow. "I'd debate you on that." He narrowed his eyes. "What happened to the little bird with the yellow bill?"

"Excuse my language, but he got his fucking head stomped."

A flicker of a smile began to brighten Banner's face. He leaned back in his chair and crossed his arms.

"You know the language all right. I never could stand a liar."

"I know what three years can teach you."

"I hear you're supposed to be some kind of bad ass?"

"I wouldn't say that."

"Other people do. Wallace told me you just got out of lockup for cutting a man."

"Yes sir. That's true."

"I also hear you've been arrested twice in the last six months for fighting?"

"That's also true."

"And you don't call that a bad ass?"

"Well," Billy drawled, forcing back a smirk. He looked up sharply. "I ain't been whipped yet."

"You ain't been whipped yet, eh?" Banner leaned over his desk. "So you haven't been beaten yet." He stared at the application. "Well, I'll tell you what, Mr. Riley. I'm going to give you a week's trial period." He paused to let the statement sink in. Billy nodded.

"I've got a feeling it's not going to be easy for you to work here. Most of my customers are from Haymont and snooty as hell—doctors and lawyers, members of Highland Country Club. You're going to have to suck ass and smile like a fool."

"I'd appreciate any work you can give me."

"There's worse things a man can do than fight. I'd like to think

I've never been whipped, neither." Banner pointed at a cloth folded on a shelf.

"You can get started by wiping your nose grease off the front window."

BILLY spent the first couple of days watching Banner please his customers, feeding the white rats on Purina Dog Chow, and changing the soggy newspaper flooring the puppy cages twice a day. During slack times, Banner showed him how to work the cash register and record the day's receipts. He watched Billy hawkishly, and was quick to find fault and correct with the impatience that comes of years in the military. The work was boring, only made tolerable to Billy by memories of his week without the sun.

On the fifth day, Friday, Banner put Billy behind the cash register.

"Just think first, always. Count change carefully."

Billy's first sale was to a man who only wanted meal worms for his lizard collection. Billy talked him into buying a horned toad just in from Arizona. Later, a fortyish-aged woman came in looking for a rhinestone collar for her cat. She was ten pounds too heavy for the revealing dress she wore, a large cocktail diamond ring shimmering on one finger.

"Take a look at these kittens, ma'am," Billy said, lifting a furry Persian from a box. The woman cooed, holding the young male against her face.

"I don't want to sound fresh, ma'am, but you two look like a shot out of a *Playboy* magazine."

Banner smiled while Billy rang up the sale. By closing time, Billy had made seven sales on his own, using the broad smile he was born with, and the slick tongue that came from growing up on the east side.

"I reckon we'll say your trial period is over," Banner said after the front door was locked. He handed Billy a key. "I trust a man just as far as he will let me. You open up Monday morning at eight."

Billy left the shop walking light, his first week's wages stuffed deep in a front pocket. A few celebration beers would taste good, he thought.

Billy walked down the hill from Haymont, toward Hay Street in the center of town. Three of the blocks were crowded with topless bars, tatoo parlors, neon lights and street-corner prostitutes—the local gathering place for soldiers from nearby Fort Bragg.

At the end of one block, Billy entered a bar he frequented called the Cuddle-Up. The bar was small and dark and quieter than many of the larger bars where drunk soldiers often fought. He took one of the tables in the corner. Black lamps hung from the ceiling and shone on walls painted with crude pictures of unicorns, dragons and futuristic warriors. The soft light rounded the edges of the tables and chairs, and caused specks of lint on his oxford shirt to glow like fireflies.

"What you have, honey?" asked the waitress in tight, black leotards and a short, white leather skirt. Her mascara was beginning to run where her eyes watered from cigarette smoke. She bent to wipe the table with a wet cloth.

"Hey, Lilly," Billy said. "Ya'll have draft tonight?"

"Yeah," she said, popping her gum.

"Bring me a couple."

The music started up again, loud and throbbing from two large speakers that hung above the dancer's ramp. The next dancer up appeared from out of a back room and was helped onto the stage by two eager soldiers. She slowly untied her haltertop, viewing herself in a full-length mirror at the back of the ramp, then hung the garment on a nail in the wall. Billy studied her—late twenties maybe, full breasts that jiggled nicely as she danced. Too nicely, probably silicon. Wearing only a spangled G-string, her legs long and oiled and thin, a cesarean scar showed on her belly. She flashed her brilliant, fake smile as she pranced down the stage, moving fluidly, snake-like, gaz-ing soulfully into the eyes of the young men crowding the stage. Occasionally she tweaked her nipples to make them stand out. Dollar bills she saw in their eyes, crisp greenbacks anyone could stuff under the band of her G-string by hand, foot or mouth. She tweaked and twirled and beckoned, fucking the soldiers with her eyes, taking their money, then whirling away, leaving them only a wink, a smile and a hard-on.

Billy shook his head, sipped his beer, and felt very wise and worldly for not being sucked in by her lie. A succession of women followed, all nearly identical in their methods, while Billy watched, drinking beer after beer. He was standing to leave when the quiet dancer came on, younger, red hair braided down her back nearly to her waist, slender to the point of being skinny, small high breasts, and green eyes that looked fiercely beyond the leering men to a place Billy could only imagine.

6

RUBY looked hardest at the new drivers. One by one, dozens of regulars had proven to be just another ride. Still, she brought fresh hope to the job each day, thinking maybe tonight her luck would change, that this one would really love her and take her away to the wonderful places she imagined around the next curve. With this eternal spark of optimism, she greeted the black-haired man who came into the diner thirty minutes before she went off shift. He looked to be in his early fifties, with a rough-cut jaw and unusually white teeth in his smile.

"What you having tonight, cowboy?" Ruby asked, holding a note pad and pencil in one hand. "House special is mighty good."

"You wouldn't be the house special, would 'ya?" He grinned broadly.

"Honey, I'm worth a hell of a lot more than two dollars and fifty cents." She gave him a solid punch on the shoulder. Her eyes traced down his arm to a hand that was thick and calloused. No wedding band, she noticed. "Where you come from, any-way, cowboy?" she asked with encouragement. "I ain't seen you around here before."

"Been hauling between D.C. and Chicago. This is the first time I've been on this run."

"Well, welcome in." Ruby flashed her best grin. "In a month's time you'll be swearing that this is the best hash house on I-95."

"It's got the prettiest women. I already see that."

"Sweetheart, you'll find that flattery will get you everywhere with me." She slapped his back and began writing up his order. At the kitchen window, she shouted "the works" at the cook, trying to drown out the voice that was already echoing inside her head.

Cut it out, Ruby. What's any man ever brought you but tears in the end? What can this one give you that you haven't hurt for a hundred times?

"Hash with the works," Ruby said louder. She began filling a glass with crushed ice. Her actions were nearly frantic, as she spilled ice on the counter and onto her dress. She poured tea, then stirred in two large spoonfuls of sugar. Starting back towards the man, she watched him watch her, trying to walk lovely as possible with twenty extra pounds in a grease-stained uniform.

"You like it sweet, don't you?" Ruby asked, a little out of breath. "You like your tea with lots of sugar?"

"How'd you know that?" he smiled. "I like it sweeter than soda pop."

"I just thought you might." Ruby felt her face flushing. "You just strike me as the type who likes it real sweet." She whirled around and started for the kitchen where the cook was already yelling "plate."

A little plump, the man thought, watching Ruby walk away. But friendly. Mighty damn friendly.

"Linda, how about watching my section a minute," Ruby called to one of the other waitresses. She walked into the ladies' room and closed the door. From a shelf over the mirror, Ruby took down a small cosmetic case. She leaned forward and studied her reflection. She wore very little makeup, and in the fuzzy light of the neon bulb, her face looked round and soft. Girl-like. Ruby always winced when she thought of her childhood.

She was born on Valentine's Day, weighing nine pounds and nine ounces, overweight then and ever since. But I was pretty, Ruby recalled, pink ribbons in my hair and a short, fluffy frock that mother dressed me in. Mike was proud of me, his only baby sister, and Bubble, he was only three, but had a curious interest, and according to his mood, would pinch me or kiss me. I was a daddy's girl, had to be with Mama dying so young. Papa's lap was broad and warm, a good place to read a storybook. His arms were thick from years of hard work in the mill. I could fall to sleep cradled there and he would carry me to bed.

Being fat wasn't so bad then, Ruby thought, and slowly shook her head. All little girls were supposed to be fat. Papa said so. Boys, they were no thought then; they were too involved in playing baseball or catching frogs on the sandbar in the river.

Ruby powdered her face. Some of the softness left, and she looked older. She remembered starting school and the beginning of names—Fat Ruby, Fattie, Big Bones, Tubby.

"Red Rover, Red Rover, send Ruby right over." And she would start toward the other team, shimmying as she ran. She'd hit the other line, and all the boys would take exaggerated falls, crying hilariously that a freight train had passed. So many jokes about getting "fat germs," the Valentine days that passed with her sack empty on the wall except for a card from the teacher.

Then Daddy died, that great refuge from the world buried six feet under cold dirt. There was still Mike. Good, brave Mike, always quick to pound anyone pulling her hair or calling her names. Remember how he'd get whipped taking on the Bain boys three at a time? He still waded in there the next time, slinging knuckles, biting, cussing and kicking; he gave it back the best he could. And Bubble. He wasn't much at fighting, but he had a soft shoulder to cry on and a soft, sympathetic voice.

Ruby traced her lips with bright red lipstick. At puberty, her friends slimmed down, grew taller and developed hard, little breasts, helped along with wads of tissue. But she just got broader, her hips fanning out, her breasts much too large for a twelve-year-old. Pimples—they thrived, large and red. All the rumors circulated that she was pregnant though she had never kissed a boy.

When she was fifteen Larry came along, that slow-talking farm boy from down in Robinson County.

Ruby had to smile at her reflection, even if the memory of Larry hurt. The years with him had been so dear.

Larry was so tall and skinny, with those huge feet and hands, and eyes that were slightly crossed. Ham Hock, they called him. Tator Head, Larry the Bumpkin, Toe-baccor.

Ruby felt for him with all her heart. And he had an eye for her, and kind words on slow walks home from school. The job he took in the mill after giving up on school gave him spare change to buy her sodas at the corner drugstore. The valentine he gave her was so large she had to hold it in both hands, along with a box of candy and bottle of toilet water. That night on the banks of the river, she gave herself to him with no regrets. The next week she quit school.

Oh, how Mike objected. He was the man of the house and tried to talk her out of it, said one day she would be sorry not to have a high-school degree.

But love was the only education that mattered. The next week they married and moved into a little apartment over the feed store. Just three rooms, but she made it nice with vases of wild flowers and curtains made from scraps of cloth Larry brought home from the mill. Those first six months were like something from a movie; the two of them had so much bottled-up love to give.

Ruby pursed her lips and dabbed at the corner of her mouth with toilet paper. She brushed on rouge and thought on.

Then came the first miscarriage. Larry kissed away most of the pain; she tucked the rest in the back of her heart. Life went on, a job at the truck stop while Larry pulled overtime at the mill.

A year passed before the second pregnancy, but she lost that one too. Mike and Bubble came home from the war. A third conception.

She wanted this child so bad. Wanted it enough to quit

working and stay off her feet. Then the night came that Larry was promoted and arrived home smiling and bragging. Two weeks later he brought home his first big check and went out for a beer, something he hardly ever did, and got locked up for disturbing the peace. From there the details were never clear, except there was a fight in the cell and Larry pulled a box cutter from his shoe to cut the man who laughed at his nose, then the flash of another blade, and Larry went down and died before they could get him off the floor.

Later that night, she lost the baby girl, the one she would have named Rose.

Ruby finished her makeup, then studied her face. No child here, she thought. Not even a young lady, but every bit a woman of forty-eight. Ruby placed her tube of lipstick and compact back in the case.

She wanted the black-haired trucker out front. For all the pain it caused her to remember the past, it always soothed her guilt to think of Larry. He would forgive her.

The man cleaned his plate, then finished up with pie and coffee, and left Ruby a two-dollar tip. He was waiting outside when she punched out, and after a few minutes of talk, they left together in Ruby's car. Already, his hand was resting on her arm.

7

THE room was small and dark. Just a desk and two chairs. On the desk sat a clock turned face down, a pen stand and an open notebook under a gooseneck lamp's orb of yellow light.

The psychologist behind the desk looked thoughtfully at Billy, tapping his forehead lightly with the eraser end of a pencil.

Billy felt uncomfortable and shifted his weight from side to side. But he sat defiantly, reared back against the slats, his arms crossed, and stared at the doctor.

"What are you angry at, Billy?"

"I'm not angry at nothing, except having to come here. Like I'm some kind of kook."

"No one is saying you're a kook, but I do think you're angry at more than just having to be here. At some person, maybe?"

"Look, Doc. I'll say it ten times if you want me to. I'm not mad at you, the world, the man in the moon, or anything else."

"O.K., once is enough. You said it and I believe you."

The doctor tapped his temple again, crossed and uncrossed his legs. "So, you're not mad at anything or anybody, and there is nothing else bothering you. We know that much."

"Yeah, I know it."

"No, we know it."

Billy shrugged. He leaned forward and lifted the clock. Only ten minutes had passed since he arrived. He lay the clock back on its face, then stared at the blade of sunlight leaking through the partially closed blinds. He rubbed his nose, then settled back in the chair, fingers beating a rapid tempo on his trouser leg. Suddenly, he sat straight again.

"O.K., Doc, you know? Maybe there is one thing I don't like. Wanna hear it?"

"What's that?"

"Rats. I've never liked goddamn rats."

"Well, a lot of people don't like rats, Billy." He scribbled on a pad of paper.

"Maybe so. But you keep wanting to hear something I don't like, so I named one."

"Rats are a good choice. I'm not terribly fond of rats myself." The doctor leaned forward a little trying to bring the conversation to a more intimate level. "Do you ever kill rats, Billy?"

"Kill 'em? Naw. Not unless they get in the house or something."

"So you never hunt them down, or trap them for the purpose of killing them?"

"I said I just don't like them, that's all. That don't mean I'm a pervert when it comes to rodents."

The doctor chuckled. "All right. You don't cut off their heads and wear them around your neck."

"You got it."

The doctor lowered his head further, and looked into Billy's eyes. "But you like people, don't you? You say there's not a single person in the world who you hold a grudge against?"

Billy slowly nodded.

"Yet some people you cut. People you have no problem with or a grudge against. I don't understand."

Billy shuffled his feet. He looked back at the blinds and wished he was outside in the sun.

BUBBLE'S sudden realization of how fast the cash inside his mattress was dwindling drove him back to his old hobby of building birdhouses. He resolved to limit his drinking to the evenings and began to devote several hours each day toward earning enough money to carry on his campaign. He poked around in the tool shed, found his jigsaw and toolbox, and was glad he hadn't pawned them. Bubble had always had a knack for woodcraft, enjoyed the smell of sawdust, the clean feel of newly milled lumber. The hobby had helped him through some slack times in the past.

Bubble sifted through a pile of rotting lumber in his backyard, killing five black widows, finally selecting six planks of wood that had the right smell, color and grain. He toted them one by one to the front porch steps where he could watch people passing while he worked.

Bubble was an hour into his work, and had paused for "just one beer—I swear to God," when Billy hopped the wire fence and strode up the cracked, concrete walkway.

"Building a boat, old man?" he asked.

"Nope," Bubble answered over the top of his can. "Martin houses." He set his half-drained can in a cooler.

"Man with two years of college ought to be able to do better than a martin house."

"You ever hear of supply and demand?"

"Can't say it's something I dwell on."

"It's one of those college things. Come November, the birds will start flying in here from up north, and people are gonna be wanting bird houses for their pretty little yards. Folks ain't going to be boating until next summer."

"So it's a matter of capital here?"

"Got to pay the rent, you know."

"Want to sell me a beer? For hard cash."

"Beer you can have. Just no wine." Bubble fished in the cooler and handed Billy a tall Budweiser. He refused the dollar. Billy sat on the steps and popped the tab. The beer was cold and no foam spewed.

"You been to church?" Bubble asked. "You're dressed like you gave the sermon."

Billy took a long swallow of beer. "Worse. I've been to see a shrink."

Bubble grunted and helped himself to another beer. "A shrink, eh? He tell you you're crazy?"

"I think he suspects so."

"All the Rileys are a little crazy. Is this some of Wallace's bullshit?"

"Yep. The judge said I had to see a shrink or stay in jail."

"I think I'd rather stay in jail. What'd you talk about?"

"Rats. I told him I don't like rats, and he told me I ought not to cut people. He thinks I ought to cut rats instead."

"You shouldn't be cutting nothing, unless it's a pork chop."

"Goddamn it, Bubble. Half the people in this town run around cutting and punching each other. Look at the Johnsons and Bains and Basses."

"Yeah, but you're a Riley. What's the Johnsons and Bains and Basses ever been but drunks and whores. 'Cept for Wallace."

"I just don't like being singled out."

"You ain't being singled out. You nearly killed a man. You're lucky to be free."

Bubble finished his beer and stared at the cooler. "Just one last beer till tonight," he said to Billy. "Got to be sensible about drinking."

"Hand me another," Billy said.

"Just one more for you, too. You get crazy when you drink."

They drank in silence until a mongrel dog passed. "You still with the pet store?" Bubble asked.

"Yeah."

"Ya'll need some birdhouses? I can make feeders too."

"Maybe. I'll ask the boss."

"Tell him I do good work." Bubble set down his beer, picked up a plank and began sawing. Billy watched the damp sawdust dribble into a tiny pile on the dirt. Bubble's red cheeks puffed out like bellows as he pushed and pulled the saw.

"What's Ruby up to?" Billy asked as the end of the plank

creaked, then fell to the ground. "You seen her today?"

"Nope. She's entertaining." Bubble mopped his forehead with a handkerchief. "She don't like me around when she's got a man on the premises."

"A man? How you know somebody's there?"

"Saw his shirts hanging on the clothesline. 'Roadway' big as hell."

Billy shook his head and spit on the ground. "You'd think a woman as good as Ruby could get better than some over-the-hill road jock. She ain't met one yet that stayed longer than a week."

"Go tell her that. You're the only one in the world she gives a shit about, anyway. Go tell her she's a damn fool." Bubble began sawing again.

Billy set his empty can on the porch, leaving a dollar folded underneath. "See you around, Bubble." When he hit the street, he turned to see Bubble reaching for his third beer.

On the corner two teenaged boys leaned against a telephone pole. They called to Billy and threw up their arms in a salute. Both had rolled their shirt sleeves above their elbows, the way Billy liked to do.

Harold Crumpler was the black-haired trucker's name. He sat on Ruby's couch with his feet resting on a cushion, sipping a beer. The television was on, and he was rooting for the Chargers over the Patriots. Ruby was cooking a late breakfast, still wearing a housecoat and scruffy, beaded bedroom slippers. She hummed softly while tending to the food, glancing occasionally at Harold's arm draped along the back of the couch, darkened with coarse, black hair. In the pan, fatty bacon sputtered pop-pop like rain on the roof.

She had him, at least for the rest of the day. The ghosts couldn't complain when she had a live one. They could shout and rage, calling her a dumb whore while she stumbled over her feet in front of a stranger, or cried after he left, but while she had him, his bare chest only a few feet away, what could dead people say?

"You want another beer, honey?" Ruby called above the touchdown roar.

"Yeah. How 'bout one more?" he said, not moving his eyes from the running back dancing in the end zone.

Ruby brought him the beer, bending to kiss the side of his head. With one hairy-knuckled hand, he patted her broad behind. Suddenly, Ruby heard the creak of the porch step, footsteps, then a rap on the front door. She quickly moved away from Harold and peeked through the window curtain. When she saw Billy she sighed.

"Who's that?" Harold asked, turning from the game.

"Just my nephew. My oldest brother's boy, Billy." She walked heavily toward the front door, paused, looked down at her pink, quilted housecoat, then at Harold's hairy chest. Ruby opened the door partway.

"Hey, sweetheart," she said hoarsely, using her girth to block the opening. "What you up to today?"

"Nothing special. You sick? You're still in your bedclothes."

"No, I'm all right." Her forced smile became strained and brittle.

Billy saw the pain in her face and eyes, and felt mean. "Hey, maybe I ought to come back later. I see you have company."

"How'd you know someone was here?"

Billy nodded toward the yard. "Unless you're the one driving for Roadway? Look, I'll drop by tomorrow."

"No. You come on in and have something to eat." Ruby reached for his arm, ashamed she had tried to deceive him. "Come on in. I'd like you to meet him, anyway."

Harold was watching from the couch. He stood awkwardly as Billy approached, then stuck out his hand.

"Pleased to meet you. I'm Harold Crumpler."

Billy took his hand and shook it firmly, much harder than was necessary. He stared into Harold's face.

"I was expecting you to be a little fellow," Harold said, grinning stiffly.

"Ain't nothing little about me, except my patience," Billy answered. He dropped Harold's hand.

Ruby stood to one side, wringing the collar of her bathrobe. Suddenly, she hugged Billy, and pecked him on the cheek. "This here is my sweetie," she announced to Harold. She turned Billy to her. "Now what you want to eat? I'll just throw in a bit more bacon and fry up some eggs in no time."

"This lady is some kind of cook," Harold said, still trying to smile.

"Yeah, I know," Billy answered. "I've only been knowing her all my life." He looked past Harold's shoulder to the television screen. "Who's winning?"

"Chargers by a field goal," Harold answered.

"Harold used to play football," Ruby said. "Didn't you, Harold?"

"Wasn't much to it. Just a little in school."

Billy stepped across the room and flopped down in a chair, hooking one leg over the armrest. Ruby hurried to the stove while Harold hiked up his trouser cuffs and sat back down. The next play was a third-and-long, and the two men watched in silence till the running back was stopped behind the line.

"So, you drive for Roadway?" Billy asked.

"Yeah. Been with them fifteen years now."

"You on long haul or local?"

"Right now, long haul. Running between Washington and Florida. I'm hoping to get on local 'round here if I can. Man my age needs to start slowing down."

Ruby smiled to herself in front of the stove. She was cracking eggs into a frying pan. "You want a beer, Billy?" she called.

"No. Takes an alkie to drink beer this early." He glanced at Harold's can sitting on the coffee table. Harold shuffled his feet. The men watched the game in silence until Ruby called them to eat. Billy ate quickly, mumbled his thanks, then rose to leave.

"You don't have to go so soon," Ruby told him. "Sit down and watch the rest of the game."

"Naw, I need to be going." He folded his arms around Ruby's

neck. "I sure think a lot of this woman," he said to Harold. "You be sweet to her."

"I think a lot of her too," Harold said.

Billy was almost to the front gate before Ruby caught up with him and grabbed his arm.

"You didn't have to act that way," she said, her eyes shiny. "He ain't like you think."

"He's a long-haul trucker, ain't he? How many times have I seen you crying over one of those guys?"

"I'm a grown woman, Billy. And I'm getting older and fatter every day."

"I just don't like to see you get hurt. You deserve a lot better."

"Give him a chance, O.K.?"

"That's up to him. The longer he keeps on coming back, the friendlier I'll be."

Billy had barely crossed the street before his anger subsided, and he began to feel guilty. At the fish market, he bought a bouquet of cut flowers from an old woman. He returned to Ruby's, laid the flowers in front of the door, knocked twice and bounded away.

While working, Bubble helped himself to four more "last beers," but still managed to saw and nail together five respectable martin houses. The evening was cooling when he sat on the steps, contemplating his work and the colors of paint he would use the next day. Passing in front of the house, slowly walked old leather-faced Cappy Pearson, dressed in rags and as usual, talking out of his head.

When younger, Cappy had worked as a dogcatcher for the county, but wine had gotten the better of him, so much that he no longer even hung around Willie's, but stayed to himself. He slept on benches or under people's cars, panhandled when sober enough, and chased imaginary dogs when drunk. As he passed, he looked at Bubble and lifted one finger to his lips. He pointed ahead to a bare spot on the sidewalk, while lengthening and slowing his stride.

"Bulldog," he hissed at Bubble.

Bubble frowned and shook his head. Kill myself before I got that bad, he thought. Blow my damn brains out.

Not with a gun, you won't, Bubble. The words trickled through his brain. Alcohol will kill you by and by just as surely.

Bubble cocked his head and listened, as if his thoughts were the tune of a distant radio. No Bubble, not as quickly or cleanly as a gun. No explosion, no easy way out.

Bubble watched Cappy stumble down the sidewalk.

What is this crazy notion of yours, anyway, the voice asked. Gonna drink all the wine in the world. Anyone can see right through it, that you've finally given up completely; it's a good cover, a noble campaign to say it's for Billy, to show him just how disgusting a drunk can be, so that maybe before he goes too far, he will draw back and examine himself and see where he is heading. It is a pretty good cover, and you halfway believe it yourself, loving him the way you loved his mother.

Blowing out your brains would be a great finale. You could write a suicide note telling your secret, and everyone would pity you and understand then why your once promising life ended with a sucession of empty bottles. Suicide is the habit of artists, and you have always known you had the heart of an artist.

But, wine will sap that last bit of pride before it will give you the courage or numbness to pull the trigger. The DT's will spread their tentacles throughout your brain, as they have already done to Cappy and a thousand other men on the east side.

Bubble bumped his forehead with his fist to dislodge the bad thoughts. Cappy stepped from the curb and stumbled across the street.

BUBBLE RILEY was born ass first on a windy February day in 1924. Because of the breech, he was in the chute several hours longer than normal, finally squeezing out lop-headed and blue. Life was shallow for several days.

But, Bubble kept on squawling. That's probably why he lived, having to breath in order to cry.

Mike was already four, and independent for one so young. He found little threat in such a wrinkled, ugly, yelling thing as Bubble.

Then Ruby came when Bubble was three, that pink, cooing round bundle that immediately took his spot on his mother's lap. Bubble learned quickly that the nest ended very early. He resorted to thumb-sucking, standing forlornly by his mother's knee, blanket in hand. Big, hard-working Daddy ended that campaign by burning the blanket and putting Texas Pete on his son's thumb.

Bubble carried on the war underground, sucking his thumb in the closet, wetting his pants until he was seven and pinching hunks out of Ruby when no one was around.

Bubble was named Charles at birth, but owed his nickname to Mike. Bubble constantly had gas, and Mike would laugh so loud when the bubbles boiled around the flanks of his younger brother while being bathed.

Bubble soon found that Mike was good at more than name-calling—he excelled in stickball, kick-the-can, tree climbing, racing and most any other competition between young boys. Bubble found out nearly as early that he was not athletic. He was usually the last or next-to-last person picked for teams, and got thumped on his head by the Bains and Johnsons nearly as much as he was picked on by Mike.

In time, Bubble did find there was one area where he excelled over his brother and most of the kids on the east side. The classroom. He held that bit of pride like a cocked gun inside his head.

BUBBLE watched Cappy disappear around the corner of the block. "Yep, blow my goddamn brains out first," he insisted, drowning out the tiny voice of his conscience.

Bubble stood, grimacing from his stiff back, then began placing his tools under the shelter of the porch. He carefully oiled the saw blade, then settled back in his rocker with a favorite blue tin cup and a fifth of wine. He drank the first two cups mixed half and half with 7-Up, felt the warm numbness of a high settling over his mind, then changed to drinking straight wine. He ate a can of beans and franks and a pack of cheese nabs, tuned his radio to a classical station in Chapel Hill, slumped in his chair, and by nine-thirty was belly-laughing drunk.

Soon his head began to nod as he settled into a stupor. The dream began, Mike's image flickering in the bushes like a candle flame, growing brighter until it shone the green of fireflies.

"What the hell you want?" Bubble asked, squinting one eye. In his dream, he sat higher, wondered how Mike could return, took a long swallow from his bottle. Mike still stood before him when he looked again. "Why you nosing around here?"

"Looking at a damn drunk." Mike grew brighter when he spoke.

"Least I'm living." Bubble made another effort to sit straight. "I'm still sucking down wind."

"You'll be with me soon enough," Mike replied. "Damn soon if you keep drinking like this."

"What's it matter? Dying ain't nothing but just another thing."

Mike fluttered, as if losing energy. "Just know you're dying for that bottle of wine. Forget that crap about dying for Billy."

"Somebody's got to die for him, else he's done for."

"I've already done the deed."

"Naw, brother. You died for that goddamn mill."

"I died for Billy. He's my boy and can't no one else die for him."

"Don't be so sure."

Mike fluttered again and dimmed, then left like smoke on a rising breeze.

A passing car backfired, and Bubble jerked awake. He stared into the shadows of the bushes, saw only stems and leaves, then held his bottle of wine to the light. "Crazy-making wine for sure. Hell of a dream." He drained what was left in the bottom. "Foolish-making wine. Can't let Billy drink this stuff."

Soon, Bubble passed out, his chin dropping to his chest. The bottle slowly slipped from his fingers and rattled on the porch boards.

Billy came by after midnight on his way home from a bar. Bubble was snoring loudly, a long dribble of saliva coursing down his chin. Billy helped himself to a beer in the cooler, then sat watching the older man's chest rise and fall with long, slow breaths. Billy frowned, felt his good high slipping into sadness. After half his beer, he tossed the can and tried to wake Bubble, but got only groans. He carried a blanket from the house and covered him, tucking it carefully around his feet. Then Billy left, walking heavily, sighting on streetlights ahead to keep from appearing too drunk.

8

BILLY'S second week in the pet shop passed like the first, though he learned the price of most common items and could stop looking in the book. Banner still watched him, but, as the days passed, spent more and more time on inventory or long lunch breaks. Friday morning arrived before Billy could believe it. As he daydreamed at the counter about the weekend, Banner stopped on his way to a dental appointment.

"There's this guy who will probably come by about ten," he said. "I thought I ought to mention him."

"My parole officer?"

"No, nothing like that. Guy brings in his snake to be fed."

"Yeah? So what you want me to do? Cram a hamburger down it's throat?"

"All you have to do is sit the cage in a back room and drop a rat in. He'll come back later and you charge him $2.50."

"I reckon I can handle that."

Banner left. Billy wasn't afraid of snakes. While in college, Bubble had taken a biology course and learned how to identify many of the local species of snakes. On fishing trips, he had taught Billy. Billy had even kept a few nonpoisonous snakes when he was a kid.

So, it wasn't fear that stirred his belly now. The feeling was new and strange.

The morning passed slowly, only a few customers coming in. Billy was leaning over the counter reading a paper when a middle-aged man wearing a suit came in carrying a plywood cage with a glass front. Billy watched with interest while the man set the cage on the floor.

"Dave Banner here?" he asked.

"He's gone to the dentist. Don't worry, he said you were coming."

The man frowned.

"Look, I know about snakes. I've even kept a few. What kind you have in there?" Through the glass, Billy could see only a dark mass.

"Boa constrictor."

"One rat?"

"Yeah, but not too large."

"No problem. By the time you get back, he'll be burping."

After the man left, Billy kneeled and peered through the glass. He was startled by the size of the snake, probably five feet long and thick as his forearm. He carried the cage to the back room, the snake lying as still as if molded from clay. Then he walked to the rat cage, walking deliberately as if entering a church.

The rats met him at the wire, always happy to see humans and the food pellets they often brought. Billy took a handful of the pellets from a sack and dropped them in the food pan. The rats scrambled, their pink, hairless tails twitching while they ate.

Billy stood watching, trying to decide which rat to use. He felt curious and God-like while debating which rats should live and which one should die. He also felt childlike, as if fishing for brim and deciding which worm to impale on the hook. Since they seemed to be the same size and weight, Billy decided to at least be democratic in the selection. He took a garden glove off a shelf and slipped it over his right hand. Then he reached into the cage and began stirring the rats.

The rats clustered around his hand, seeking more food. Billy turned his head from the rats, then closed his fingers around one. "Oh ye chosen one," he whispered, drawing it from the cage.

The Biblical tone seemed appropriate. At first, the rat struggled, its red eyes bulging, but then settled to breathing rapidly. Billy inspected it—average—no fatter or leaner, its quick heart thumping against his glove. He carried the rat to the snake's cage.

The boa, still lying in the same coil, seemed to take no notice when Billy waved the rat in front of the glass. He opened the small door on top, took a deep breath, then dropped the rat inside. Billy knelt quickly in front of the glass.

Billy had expected the boa to strike instantly, burying its teeth in the rat, then drawing the rat into steel-like coils. But the rat simply plopped on the floor, sat up to twitch his nose, then began to slowly amble around the cage. The boa lay with his tongue flicking frequently, but otherwise showed no interest. The rat sniffed towards the head of the snake. Billy held his breath, while the rat continued, interested in the strange odor. The rat paused at the edge of the coils, sniffed twice, then began crawling over the boa.

"Stupid damn rat," Billy whispered. The rat had never seen a snake before and harbored no natural fear. He scrambled over the lukewarm coils, even stepping on the boa's head. The boa simply drew his head back as if annoyed. Billy had to remind himself to breathe, but the rat, unharmed, continued over the snake, then waddled across the sawdust to the far side of the cage. Billy shook his head.

The sound of the front door opening announced another customer. Billy heard steps. He watched the rat sit on his back legs licking his forepaws. The snake still seemed unconcerned. Billy stood and dusted off his knees, then went into the store. A customer was standing by the counter.

"Sorry," Billy said. "I was doing some things in the back."

"You have any guppies?" the man asked.

Guppies, Billy thought. Here I'm trying to watch a miracle of nature and the man wants guppies. "Sure we do," Billy said. "We have two tanks full."

With a sweep of his hand, Billy showed the man what was

available. The man stooped to look. Suddenly, from the back room, Billy heard a thump, then a squealing sound. The squeal stopped after a couple of seconds.

"Three for five bucks?" the customer asked.

"Yeah," Billy answered, staring towards the back room. The room was silent.

"Give me six," the customer said.

Billy worked fast, trying to mask his impatience. Soon as the man left, Billy hurried to the back room.

The rat was gone. On the sawdust was a damp spot where the rat had emptied his bowels from fright. The boa had resumed his coils and looked the same except for a thickening in the middle. Billy shuddered. God, he thought, if there is such a thing as reincarnation, let me next time come back as a snake.

THE day passed quicker with the arrival of the money-bearing Friday customers. Banner closed the front door promptly at eight, checked up, paid Billy and sent him on his way. Billy headed downtown towards the bar district.

He hadn't forgotten the red-headed dancer from the week before. Something about her stuck in his mind, how frail she seemed, the intense way she stared beyond the faces of the men. He felt silly over going to see a dancer who probably would not notice him, but still he hurried down the street, telling himself that the bar had the best draft in town.

Mid-month had arrived, soldier's payday, and the street was crowded. Billy tried to ignore the roar of car engines and shouts from people passing. That week in the county jail was still fresh in his mind.

The bar was more crowded than usual, but Billy found a table against one wall. A dancer was strutting to a Mick Jagger song, squatting occasionally for men to stuff bills in her G-string. The money rounded her abdomen like bullets in a bandolier, sweat gleaming on her skin like a coating of wax.

"Draft," Billy told the waitress. She was back soon with a tall, frosted mug. Billy drank quickly, then ordered another and settled down to watch the dancer. A couple of drunk soldiers stumbled as they passed on the way to the pisser, one even bumped Billy's arm, but he stared ahead and ignored it. He didn't want to fight. Nothing in the Cuddle-Up was worth fighting about, nothing west of the river.

Half an hour later, the green-eyed girl came on. Billy sat up straight in his chair, then stood leaning against the wall so he could see better. She folded her halter top carefully, placed it on the top step, then turned, flashed on her fake smile and glided down the ramp, stepping lightly in time to the music. Her hair was again back in pigtails, which hung down her back halfway to her buttocks. Her skin, very white between the freckles, seemed to have a transparent shine under the neon lights. She was as slender as Billy had remembered, almost skinny, with long, colt-like legs and small breasts that stood high and didn't jiggle.

Soon, Billy could see she wasn't as popular as the other dancers. Not that she couldn't dance. Even Billy could see she had style, that if anything she seemed to hold back as if something in her wanted to cut loose. But her aloofness kept her apart, her unseeing eyes and controlled steps. Even when she squatted to receive a tip, there were no lies in her eyes, but a chill that kept men from coming back.

What the hell is she doing here? Billy wondered. She looks about as comfortable up there as I would be.

His interest mounted. She finished three songs, bowed slightly, carefully tied on her top and left the stage. As she walked from the room, Billy doubted she was aware of the men staring at her, or smelled the cigarettes or stale beer. Her body had been making the motions of dance, but her mind was clearly in a distant place. She entered the small back room where the dancers dressed and closed the door.

"Who's that red-headed dancer?" Billy asked the waitress while he ordered another beer.

"New girl," she answered. "She started last week."

"What's her name?"

"I don't know. She doesn't talk much."

"How about bringing her a Coke," Billy said, handing the woman another dollar. "Ask her her name."

"O.K." The waitress cracked her gum and smiled. "You just a little sweet on her?"

"Just bring her a Coke, how 'bout?"

After a few minutes, the waitress carried a Coke into the dancer's room. When she returned, she whispered to Billy. "She said to tell you thanks."

"What's her name?"

"She said to tell you it's Pudding Tane."

"Pudding Tane, umph? Real friendly, ain't she?"

"She's that way with everyone."

Twice more the green-eyed girl danced, both times carrying the same aloofness and distance about her like a cloak. She always returned quickly to the back room, never mingling with the men like the other dancers. Billy stayed until the bar was closing. The waitress flirted a little, but he kidded her and let it pass; she was too old and made-up to appeal to him. He stood outside, sucking in the cold air and trying to get his head straight before crossing town. He had stepped off the curb when the red-headed dancer, bundled in a long coat, came out of the bar, walking quickly with her eyes turned to the pavement.

"Hey, lady," Billy said. She passed him without lifting her eyes.

"Hey, Pudding Tane," he called louder.

The girl turned to give him a long stare. "What do you want?"

"Just your name. I bought you a Coke earlier."

"About ten people a night buy me a Coke."

"Mine was the sweetest one." Billy gave her his best shy smile, and stepped closer. "Come on, Red. I'm just trying to say hello."

"I don't fuck soldiers."

"Who said anything about fucking?" Billy was taken back by her language. "I'm not a soldier, anyway."

"Your hair is short."

"I used to be a soldier."

"I don't fuck used-to-be soldiers either."

"Hey, lady, I'm not asking for nothing," Billy said, feeling his face begin to burn. "I just wanted to know your name."

"Make something up." She walked away into the night.

BY pure chance, the red-haired girl came into the pet shop the following Monday. Billy looked up from his paper at the tinkling bell, and there she was, standing in the doorway, sniffing the air as if it were peculiar. She was wearing jeans and a flannel shirt, with her hair hanging loose on her shoulders. When she spied Billy, her eyes narrowed as if trying to place him.

"Pudding Tane," Billy said and grinned. "Welcome to my humble shop."

She hesitated, then walked to the counter. "Now I remember you. You're the drunk guy who stopped me outside the bar."

"I wasn't drunk."

"You were swaying."

"We can't seem to get along, can we?"

She shrugged. "You have any birdseed?"

Billy took two boxes from the shelf behind him. "We have two types—gourmet and fast food." He laid them in front of her. She read the contents more intently than necessary.

"Why don't we start over," Billy stuck out his hand. "I'm Billy Riley and I'm sober today, and I'm not a soldier but a merchant of birdseed."

Tentatively, the girl reached out her hand to meet his. Her fingers were long and dappled with freckles.

"I'm Cassie Hicks."

"Got you!" Billy said.

She returned his smile. "Sorry if I was rude the other night. I never feel friendly after working."

"That's all right. I was a little drunk, anyway."

She withdrew her hand and began to fumble in her purse. "I'll take this one." She picked up the better brand.

"What sort of bird you have?"

"Yard birds."

The tightness between them felt like strands of rope. Billy rang up the sale, then placed the box carefully in a sack. "You from around here?"

"No. Further south."

"Out of state?"

"Yes."

"What brought you to Fayetteville?"

She sighed. "Bad luck."

As she turned to leave, Billy gathered his courage with a quick breath. "What would you think about having dinner with me tonight?"

"I have to work."

"How about afterwards?"

She moved toward the door. "I'm always very tired then."

"A cup of coffee would pick you right up."

Cassie opened the door and watched the fallen leaves tumble across the pavement. "All right, you can come after work if you want," she said. "But don't come in the bar."

"What time?" Billy felt a pleasant flutter in his stomach.

"I'm through at eleven. But remember, wait outside."

Billy watched her cross the parking lot. There was lightness in her steps.

BILLY stood outside the Cuddle-Up Lounge fifteen minutes early, nearly alone, most of the soldiers having squandered their paychecks over the weekend. He sat on the curb, checked his watch, and waited. There was no moon, and beyond the streetlights he could see the brighter stars.

At precisely eleven, Cassie came out wrapped in her long coat. Although she smiled, her face was tight and weary. "You been waiting long?" she asked.

"Just a few minutes. You look tired."

"Monday's always tough. Only three girls working."

"Sorry I don't have a car. I'm saving for one."

"It doesn't matter. The cold air feels good."

They started down the avenue toward an all-night diner. Billy's hands felt awkward, so he stuffed them in his pockets.

"Nice night, ain't it?" he finally said. "Stars are really bright when there's no moon."

Cassie looked at the sky, searching, as if noticing the stars for the first time in a long while. "I always liked those," she said, pointing toward several stars in a cluster rising over a building. "They look like a kite."

"That's Orion. The part that looks like a kite tail is supposed to be his belt."

"How do you know?"

"When I was a kid I had a telescope. See that red star? It ain't really a star. It's a planet. Mars."

"Oh," she said, making a complete turn. The chill of late night had colored her face and taken some of the weariness from her eyes. She smelled nicely of perspiration and perfume. "So, why are you selling birdseed when you know all about stars?"

"It's just a job. I don't plan to be there long."

"Me either," she echoed softly. "Me either."

Inside a diner on Bragg Boulevard, they found a booth away from the clatter of the kitchen. Billy ordered rib-eyes for them both, with french fries and salad. Cassie slowly drank her coffee, letting the steam warm her face.

"Why didn't you want me to come inside the bar?"

Cassie took another sip of coffee. "I was embarrassed, I guess. It's sort of hard to stand naked in front of someone you've just met, then later drink coffee with him."

"I think you dance pretty good."

"I dance very well. Bar dancing is just not my specialty."

"Yeah? Well, like you said, it's just a job."

They ate in silence. Billy knew the night wasn't going very well. When they had drained two cups of coffee and dropped their napkins, he offered to walk her home.

"That's not necessary. I live close by."

"No. This isn't such a good town to be walking alone late at night."

Midnight had passed. Orion, still burning brightly, had climbed high over the bank building. They zig-zagged down side streets until she stopped in front of a small basement apartment in a rooming house. Cassie stood twisting ringlets of hair around her finger.

"Thanks for the dinner. I enjoyed talking to you."

"Yeah, sure. It was my pleasure. I'm sorry we had to walk."

"Walking is good exercise. I got to see Orion, too."

"Yeah, well, maybe we'll do it again some time." He felt the awkwardness coming again and stuffed both hands in his pockets. "See you around, Cassie."

When Billy turned to leave, she reached to touch his arm. "You're not going to ask me to sleep with you, are you?" There was surprise in her voice, but her eyes held a twinkle.

"Ah, I didn't think you would want to."

"I don't. Still, guys always ask."

Billy just shrugged. "I ain't that easy." He smiled.

"You're sort of nice," Cassie said.

"Thanks. I like your freckles."

"Your hair is too short."

"It's growing out."

Cassie leaned and kissed him lightly on one cheek, said goodnight, and went inside.

BILLY had gotten used to being found attractive by women. Standing six-foot-two, lean, with good teeth and a quick, easy smile, he had found among most women of the east side, he could pick and choose. His awkwardness around Cassie bothered him. With this in mind, he ambled over to talk with Bubble the following evening after work.

Bubble was painting the last of his five new birdhouses, near enough to quitting time to be sipping from a freshly opened jug of wine. He set the bottle under the porch when Billy came through the gate.

"You ain't fooling me none," Billy said. "I've already seen your wine."

"Yeah? Well, I don't want to hear your yapping. Ruby yaps enough for the whole world."

"Somebody better yap at you. Else, you're going to drink yourself into the grave. And don't tell me, I know, you're drinking for me."

Bubble grunted as he finished the last strokes with a paintbrush. He lifted the box to the light, turned it, then set the box on newspapers to dry beside the others. Then he reached under the porch for his bottle and took a long draw, squinting at Billy while he swallowed. Carefully, he placed it back.

"Wine makes you crazy." Bubble belched, then spat on the ground. "You ain't working today?"

"Only half a day. Got off at noon."

"You can have a beer then. You want a beer?"

"No."

"If you do, look in the fridge. Are you gonna sell my birdhouses or not?"

"The boss said to bring in a few and we'll try them out."

"They'll sell. I'll bring some over tomorrow."

Billy watched the luster of the paint lessen as it dried. Bubble fumbled with his tools, arranging them in a metal box.

"I been wondering about something, Bubble," Billy said.

"Such as what?"

"What makes people do things they're not halfway suited for? Like people who work at jobs they really hate."

"Money will do it. The need for dough will make a person do most anything."

"Even dance with their clothes off?"

Bubble closed his tool box. "I'd dance naked on top of the Market House if someone paid me enough." He chuckled. "Goddamn, boy. You thinking of doing some strip-teasing?"

"No, it's this girl I met at one of the clubs downtown. She dances topless, and not only is she no good at it, but it's pretty clear she hates every second."

"Yeah? Well, as long as you and them idiot soldiers are cramming bills down her britches, she'll probably keep at it."

"I'm not cramming money down her britches. I just took her out last night after work."

"So, you were cramming something else, then?"

"Yeah, cramming my hands in my pockets. She's not the quick type."

"Well, by God, I wouldn't think she's the shy type, neither."

"Look, I'm serious, Bubble. You know how dancers are. Flirting all the time and staring in your eyes. This girl acts like she's somewhere in the clouds. Hardly even smiles."

"It's all that dope she's taking."

"It's not dope."

"Take some advice, huh? Just screw her and don't worry about what's in her mind. Life is simpler that way."

"She's different."

"She's a dancer, ain't she?" Bubble reached for his bottle. "What am I advising you for, anyway? You've never had any problem getting women. Me, I didn't even know white women had pussies till I went off to the service." He lifted his bottle while Billy laughed.

"Just go with the flow, eh?" Billy asked. "That the Bubble philosophy?"

"Yep. Use your pecker as a compass."

LATE the next night, Billy stood outside Cassie's door, debating whether to knock or walk away. Although it was past midnight, light spilled from under her door. When he knocked, he heard movement, then her voice asking who was there.

"It's me, Billy."

The door opened a crack.

"I hope you weren't sleeping," Billy apologized. "I just wanted to stop by and say hello."

"At twelve-thirty?"

"If it's too late, I'll leave."

The door opened wider till Billy could see her face. "I was practicing my yoga. I guess it's O.K. for a little while."

Cassie was dressed in a green sweat suit, her hair damp from perspiration and hanging straight. She was barefoot.

"Yoga must be pretty hard work," Billy said, noticing how the neckband of her sweat shirt was wet.

"No, yoga is like sleeping. I was practicing my dancing earlier."

Billy followed her inside. "I would think you'd get enough practice at work."

"Not that kind of dancing, silly. I do ballet."

"Oh." He glanced around her two-room apartment, sparsely furnished with only a table and chair and mattress on the floor. The walls were covered with posters of ballet dancers. The box of birdseed he had sold her sat on a windowsill. Outside the glass was a small feeder.

"You must be pretty serious about dancing," Billy said. He looked for a place to sit. "Don't have much furniture, do you?"

"I don't need much. I'm saving every penny I make so I can get out of that bar." She motioned toward the mattress. "Sit there. Imagine it's a sofa."

Billy eased himself on the mattress, the dancers towering above him. "You know all these people?"

"I know of them. I've studied their dancing, and even seen some of them perform."

"I never was much on dancing. Maybe a little rock and roll, but not this stuff."

Cassie went into the kitchen and brought back a quart bottle of Pepsi. She poured two glasses. "Sorry, but it's not very cold. I keep it outside on the windowsill."

"Don't worry about it." He took a swallow.

"You're not drinking tonight?"

"Hey, I'm not some old sot, you know. Usually, I just drink on weekends."

"You shouldn't drink at all. It wrecks your coordination."

"So, you want to be a ballerina when you grow up?"

"Yep. Ballet and modern dance. I'm very serious about it."

"Well honey, I hate to tell you this, but dancing at the Cuddle-Up ain't exactly Swain Lake."

Cassie exhaled then and shut her eyes tightly. "Swan Lake," she said in exasperation.

"I'm sorry," Billy said.

Over the next half hour, she told him she'd learned about ballet from a social worker when she was a child, of working part-time jobs after school to pay for lessons. She had left her sixth foster home the day she turned eighteen, bound for New York City, and hopefully a part with some big-time dance company. Billy understood then what she saw beyond the faces of the men.

"My purse was stolen in the bus terminal in Atlanta. I was broke as a con when I came through here. Didn't even have the price of a hamburger." Her voice lowered and quivered. "Sometimes a person has to do things they'd rather not in order to live." Her face hardened. "But there's lots worse a person can do. Lots worse."

Billy agreed, then told her about his trouble with the law. She listened with wide eyes when he told her about cutting the soldier.

"That's so bizarre! You don't seem like the type who would fight."

"I never used to. It's just something that comes over me. I feel like I'm smothering, sort of like there is a bag over my head."

Billy felt better after telling her of his trouble. The tension he had felt between them lessened greatly.

"Why don't you become a boxer?" Cassie said, then laughed. "You must have the talent."

Billy fingered a buttonhole on his shirt collar. "There's lots of things a person can be if they live to be a hundred." He lay back and stared at the ceiling. There were hundreds of fly specks. He searched for patterns that might resemble constellations. None.

"Hey Cassie," he began. "I wanna ask you something."

"So ask."

"You seem pretty sure of yourself about this dancing thing."

"If I don't believe in myself, who will?"

"But, what if you never get there? To Broadway, I mean. You really think a person can have something just by wanting it bad enough?"

"If I didn't believe that, you think I'd be baring my tits in front of half this town? I'd be selling hamburgers or punching a register at K-Mart." She pouted her mouth. "Besides, all I have to do is close my eyes, and I'm already there."

Billy propped himself up on one elbow. "I wish I could think that way. I wish to God I could."

"How old are you, anyway?" she said. "You depress me. You talk like you're seventy-five years old with terminal cancer."

"No. I'm not like you think. But, I've known a lot of people who wanted something real bad. Real damn bad. And they never got it. Some didn't even come close."

"Maybe they're just born quitters," she said, shaking her head as if to muffle his words.

Billy thought of the time that Bubble went to New York and brought home the telescope. "No, I don't know any quitters. Maybe they stop trying so hard, but they don't quit." Billy looked into Cassie's face. "I bet a hundred times my uncle told me how he was going to take me back with him to visit New York again. See all those tall buildings, and ride the subway, and eat Chinese food." Billy's voice took on a hard edge. "Now he lays up drinking wine and gets on my ass about everything. And he'll never set foot in New York again. At least not for real."

Billy sighed, then lay back on the mattress. He thought of all the bleary-eyed people on the east side, hunched over their morning coffee, trying to read some sense into the cracks on the linoleum table top, the past-due notice on the kid's hospital bill haunting their thoughts. If they didn't "want" bad enough, maybe there was a cruel power above man, something as fickle as sleeping serpents. "My telescope got missing about five years ago when Bubble was on a drunk," Billy continued. "I knew then he would never go back."

Cassie pivoted on the mattress and draped her spidery legs across his. Then she placed her fingertips over Billy's temples. "I want you to play a game with me."

"I ain't much with games."

"Come on. Think Billy. Hard. Tell me the most far-out thing you ever wanted to be."

"A girl's bicycle seat."

"Be serious, dummy. Something real. Maybe something you wanted to be when you were a kid."

Billy rolled his eyes. "O.K. A fireman."

"No. Keep going. Close your eyes."

"A six-pack. A cowboy. A cop."

"You're not there yet."

"The president. A pro basketball player. An astronomer."

"What was that?" She squeezed his arm. "What was that last thing you named?"

Billy frowned. "An astronomer? What's so strange about that?"

"Nothing's strange about it. That's wonderful!"

"What's more wonderful about being an astronomer than a cowboy?"

"Because you mean it. That's the first thing you named with any feeling in your voice."

"Hell. My throat's just dry from so much silly talking."

Cassie smiled and leaned closer to whisper. "You can be an astronomer, Billy. I can see the scientist in you oozing out all over."

"I'm no damn scientist. I'm just another rat wanting to escape the coils of serpents."

Cassie cocked her head. "You're an odd one, Billy Riley." She studied his face.

"You know," Billy said, "maybe there's something to what you say. There's something I want right now more than anything I've wanted in a while."

"What's that?" she asked.

"To kiss you."

"That's all?"

He shrugged. "That's up to you."

"Just how bad do you want to kiss me, Billy?"

"Bad enough to get right up and turn off the lights."

Billy stood and flipped the lamp switch. In the darkness, a shaft of light filtered through the blinds, illuminating one side of Cassie's face like a crescent moon.

9

RUBY was coming out the rear door of the diner with her sweater draped over her shoulders when Harold stepped from the darkness between two trailors.

"Lord Jesus," Ruby said, and slapped her bosom. "You liked to scared me to death."

"Sorry." Harold gave her a peck on her cheek. "I just pulled in and was trying to catch you before you left."

"Well, I been expecting you for two nights now." Ruby tried to stifle the glow that had begun in her eyes.

"I — I'm sorry, baby," he stammered. "I got caught up with a cancelled load down in Tampa."

Already, Larry's voice was nagging in her ear. Walk away, you dumb whore. Why don't you wise up for once? Whenever Ruby blinked, she saw little Rose, dressed in a lacy dress and patent-leather shoes, staring with shame.

"You could have called. You know I have a phone." Mike's voice started in, loud and fierce as always, much like he had talked to workers in the mill. Goddamn, Ruby! You gonna be a trucker-fucker all your life?

"I would have called you," Harold said, his voice almost pleading. "But I was trying so hard to make up lost time that I didn't stop."

Ruby choked back a sob. She lowered her head while Harold wrapped his arms around her.

"I just thought you weren't coming back." She buried her face against his shirt. He stroked her hair and gave it small kisses.

"Hey, you know I was coming back. I'm here, ain't I? Think I was gonna let a gal like you get away?"

Ruby hugged him with a desperation that slowly pushed Larry and Mike and finally even little Rose back in their graves. "Well, next time you got to stop and call me no matter what. You hear me?"

"I will, baby. You can bet I will."

Ruby pushed away, but held to his arms, searching his face to convince herself he was still the same sweet man. "How long you laying over?"

"Just tonight, but I'll be back through here over the weekend."

"Well, come on," she said, her usual note of mothering heavy in her voice. "I reckon you're starving to death. And you need a bath. Lord, I can smell that truck all over you."

At home, Ruby ran his bath water, then began frying eggs and ham while Harold soaked away the road grime. When he emerged from the bathroom, wrapped in a man's bathrobe Ruby kept handy, the table was set and the air was heavy with the aroma of coffee.

"This ain't much," Ruby apologized.

"Ain't much? Hell, it's damn near a feast."

Harold ate loudly, chewing and swallowing and blowing his coffee. Ruby touched his arm whenever she felt the presence of one of the dead ones. Afterwards, Harold belched and wiped his mouth and smiled so that Ruby wiggled in her chair. He moved to the couch to watch the end of the late-night movie, while she cleaned the dishes, whistling an old tune softly between her teeth.

"Hey babe, who's this?" Harold called from a bookcase in one corner. He was holding a framed citation with crossed American flags at the top. "Who's Mike Riley?"

"My brother," she said, turning slowly. "My oldest brother."

Harold whistled. "Sergeant Michael Riley," he read. "For valorous duty while engaged in combat in defense of his country." He tapped the glass and nodded. "Iwo Jima, umph? They don't just give away silver stars."

"We were always mighty proud of him." Ruby felt her face begin to color as Mike's presence fought to come back.

"Where's he now?" Harold asked.

"Dead. He's been dead half a year now."

"I'm sorry." He set the frame in place carefully, with noticeable reverence.

It took another hug and kiss from Harold to bring back the tune Ruby had been humming. They watched the movie credits, then Ruby faked a big yawn and asked if he was ready to turn in.

Ruby undressed in the dark as always when with a man. Harold, already under the covers, lay propped against a pillow, and as she took off her clothes, she appreciated that he was watching. In the darkness, Ruby imagined she was beautiful, younger with firm, long legs and a flat stomach below high breasts. She worked slowly, knowing he could only catch peeks when headlights passed the window. Then she slid under the covers beside him, smelling the soap scent of his neck, the hairs on his chest tickling her face. Now she could forget all the other men who had come and gone, even forgive them. They were necessary in finding this special man.

BUBBLE awoke early before dawn, still sitting slumped in the chair, bone cold and stiff. A fog covered the river, lapping over the banks and sliding through the trees. The street was gray and wet. He pulled the blanket tighter around his shoulders and sat watching the sky slowly lighten. A dove called from the river bank, another answered, and lights began to blink on in houses. Bubble slowly stood, his kneecaps popping. He scraped his tongue with his teeth, then spit over the porch railing. He pissed over the side, then went inside to brush his teeth. The eastern sky was pink when he turned into the gravel road that led down to the boat landing. The rocks were slick, and Bubble walked slowly down the steep incline before it leveled off at the water's edge. He followed a path that led along the river before opening up in a small grassy clearing beside the bank. An iron garden chair sat beside a pile of long-dead embers where someone had probably spent the night cat fishing. Bubble lowered himself to the chair.

Mollie, Mike's wife—Billy's mother—would have been fifty today. Bubble came here to the clearing each year on her birthday, only for several minutes, but time enough to always swear it was the last time. The clearing had changed as much as he and all the world had in twenty-five years. On the afternoons when he had come here with Mollie, grass covered the red-clay soil, the houses far away, wild flowers growing in the clearing. There were no charred rings or rusting beer cans. Mollie had called it their own secret place.

April 1950

BUBBLE felt ice cubes in his stomach every time he touched Mollie's arm to help her down the bank. She laughed each time she slipped, grabbing for him, awkward in her dress and backless shoes. Weaving through trees and around wild blueberry bushes, Bubble led her along the scant path that was nearly hidden by leaves from the past autumn. The day was clear and the sunshine made Bubble blink when the trees opened into the clearing. Mollie twirled, laughing, her dress rising full above her knees.

"Oh Charles," she exclaimed. "It's as beautiful as you said." Mollie stooped to pick a blue wild flower.

"Lightning burned this place out a few years back. No one ever comes here but me."

"You never told me you had a secret place, Charles. I did too, when I was little. I would climb into the linen closet and hide whenever I wanted to be alone."

Walking to the middle of the meadow, they sat on a carpet of fragrant clover. Mollie sat with her knees up, feet tucked under her dress. She began picking clover blossoms and looping them into a chain.

"Charles, did you really dance all night last week in that charity fundraiser?"

"Well, practically all night. Five A.M. had passed when the only other couple decided to call it quits. Mary was asleep on my shoulder, but I was holding her up and the judges didn't know."

"Is she pretty?"

"Mary? Yeah, sort of. She's only a friend. I met her in class."

Suddenly, Mollie tossed her handful of blossoms into the air and fell backwards into the grass, flinging her arms wide.

"Oh, it must be wonderful being in college. All the dances and parties."

"There's more tests than parties."

"Oh, I know. But the learning would be wonderful. You know so *many* things, Charles. All about music and the stars and engineering and foreign countries. You know so much more than Mi—"

"Than Mike?" Charles asked.

"Yes. Lots more than Mike, and he's four years older than you."

Charles laughed. "Mike's making money. I'm practically broke all the time."

"But there's more to life than making money, Charles." Mollie rolled on her side, propping her chin on one elbow. "Mike just—oh, I don't want to talk about it—he's just always so busy."

Charles watched her, liking the shadow cast by her cheekbone. Her eyes were bright. "Mike loves you, Mollie. That's just his way, even when he was little."

She sighed. "Oh, I know. And I love him too. Just sometimes." Mollie rolled suddenly on her stomach, resting her head on Charles' knee. "I was going to be a nurse, Charles. Could you ever imagine me a nurse?"

"Very easily. A good nurse, too."

"I would have been. I know it, I—oh, I shouldn't be complaining. I'm happy." She smiled, then looked away from Charles to the river. Charles studied her finely boned face, clear skin and full bottom lip. For weeks now he had been trying to convince himself he wasn't in love with her, that it was only a fondness for her. What could be worse than to be in love with Mike's wife. But as he watched her, his stomach churned.

Silently, Mollie watched the flowing water for more than a minute. Then she sat upright, reaching behind her back to grab a handful of clover. Quickly, she turned and rubbed the grass in his face, springing away from him, laughing and racing away.

"You little—!" Charles jumped up, spitting particles of clover from his mouth and running after her. She was nearly to the river's edge when he caught her, tackling her gently, arms around her waist. They rolled twice, Mollie's dress riding high on her thighs. Charles hesitated only a moment before kissing her. She returned the kiss with such passion that the rest came as natural as the current flowing before them.

IN all of Fayetteville, there were not two brothers who grew up to be more different than Mike and Bubble.

Mike Riley matured early, forced to become the master of the house when most boys his age were more interested in the growth rate of their pubic hair. He was not particularly gifted when it came to books, only did enough to be promoted each year, but was clever, crafty and a believer in hard work. With his pay from afternoon and weekend jobs, plus the little money from his father's pension, he kept the family fed. Mike was the type to look straight ahead at his objective, varying neither to the left or right, and go, go, go for it.

His attitude earned him three sports letters in high school. Mike was stocky, with a head of thick Irish-red hair and determination that kept him plowing ahead until he was on home plate or over the goal line. Girls loved him, not just for his athletic prowess, but his manners too. He never cussed around them like most boys; he opened doors, and kept his clothes clean and pressed. There were lots of boys on the east side who envied him or even despised him, but they generally kept their feelings private. One only had to tease Ruby or push Bubble to find that Mike Riley fought with the same discipline that controlled his life. He would get you if it took a week. All the Bains and Johnsons knew that.

Mike joined the Marines the day after the bombing of Pearl Harbor. He walked away from his job in the mill, swearing what he would do to the Japs. Ruby wept when he left on the train.

Mike endured four years of war. He grunted, crawled, took orders, shouted orders, and waded ashore in three major campaigns, getting wounded twice and winning two purple hearts, two bronze stars and finally a silver on Iwo Jima.

Mike came home a hero, the most decorated soldier from Fayetteville. The east side especially honored him. The mill hired Mike back, even started him a notch above general floor help. Inside of two months, everyone in management believed he was managerial stuff. After two years, Mike was promoted to shift foreman.

Bubble grew up on his brother's shirttail. Mike saved him a lot of black eyes, but the price in lost self-esteen was high. In sports, Bubble was all thumbs, fighting, having neither the stomach nor speed; as for girls, he avoided them. Bubble wasn't ugly; actually, in his teens he lost his baby chubbiness and became nearly handsome in his quiet, brooding way. But, any girl he ever got up the courage to talk to always seemed to swing the conversation to the achievements of his brother.

So Bubble studied. Studied those nights when Mike was playing ball or out with a girl and on weekends when other young people flocked to the boat landing for Saturday evening dances. He studied books on art and music and history and science, and could recite passages of literature as if he had written them himself. In his senior year, he graduated first in his class, and though he was picked as most likely to succeed, the honor seemed trivial beside the sports trophies Mike had left in the school's showcase.

Bubble spent his war years much differently from his brother. He still had six months of high school left when Mike packed off to the Marines. Upon graduation, Bubble joined the Air Corps. Killing people from ten thousand feet struck him as more objective, even if no less humane. After boot camp, Bubble took qualifying tests and was accepted for Officer Candidate School. Three months later, he was wearing gold bars. Mike was a PFC, preparing to ship off for the South Pacific, and for the first time in his life, Bubble felt he had bested him at something.

But while Bubble waited for overseas orders, Mike's division began island fighting. Bubble was assigned to a training center near the Great Lakes where he administered placement tests for the duration. He returned to the east side with memories of how cold the wind blew off Lake Superior.

Mike met and married Mollie Jones soon after his plant promotion. She was six years his junior and new in town, but the courtship lasted only two weeks. Mike saw immediately that she fit perfectly in his strategy—a wife and mother for his children.

Billy, christened William Thomas Riley, was born in the winter of 1954. His mother died one week later from severe internal infection. Her death wounded Mike deeper than any bullet had, but he sucked up his emotions into a carbon-hard ball that he kept deep inside his heart.

The relationship between Mike and his son was no-nonsense. When you love someone, Mike reasoned, it was a fact that should be appreciated but never exploited. He realized well the dangers of the east-side streets and reasoned with his plow-through attitude that it was only right for the older and wiser to dictate. Billy grew and matured under Mike's arm-length love but he was nurtured by the affection and embraces of Bubble and Ruby.

Billy was a gangling, shy eighteen-year-old when Mike packed him off to the Marine Corps. Mike believed a three-year hitch was the right start for any young man, and would instill in his son a respect for excellence and promotion, an asset in such an uncaring world. Billy never gave much thought to whether he wanted to join the service or not. He simply accepted the fact that Mike wanted him to, and went.

Boot camp hurried Billy in his transition from a boy to a young man. His muscles hardened and his weight increased by ten pounds. But more than physical improvement came an increased confidence in himself and his ability to use his maturing body. Billy's personality surfaced, his smile, clean sharp eyes and easy, rambling gait—all tools at his disposal.

Billy only tolerated his hitch in the service. U.S. troops were pulling out of Vietnam so Billy only played war. Cruises to the Caribbean for training were fine, but the discipline and polish of the Marines were another thing. He patiently but eagerly awaited his discharge. The day was eclipsed by Mike's death just three weeks prior.

For all the strengths that Mike Riley possessed, a strong heart was not one of them. The weakness showed up when Mike was forty-nine. First he experienced only a tightness in his chest that came and went, but later in a routine physical, the problem showed up. Angina, the doctor said, in the early stages, but an illness that needed to be taken care of. Only weeks before Mike had been promoted to general floor manager, quite an accomplishment for an east-side kid with only a high-school education. Slowing down was not something Mike was used to, especially not now when the things he wanted from life were within reach. He had nearly paid off the piece of land across the river in the rolling hills where the nice people lived. Two, three more years, he would clear the debt, then mortgage part of it and finance his house, a brownstone with ceder paneling and a workshop out back. It would be a fine place to leave Billy, and he could live cleanly and comfortably as he grew old, knowing he had won. Asking Mike to slow down was like asking him to give up a dream he had worked so hard for.

So he plowed on, the tightness over the years becoming a crushing pain that would double him over his desk. Everyone told him to take it easy, that at his position he didn't need to push so hard. Ruby told him, the doctor did, Bubble, the plant supervisor, even Billy in the last few months when his confidence had raised to the point where he could finally look his father unwaveringly in the eye during weekend passes. But, slowing down was a term Mike couldn't accept, and when the heart attack came it was fatal, turned his skin black and dropped him so quickly one would have thought he had been decapitated.

Mike was buried with full military honors beside his wife at the age of fifty-five. The next week, Billy was arrested for the first time.

Billy was hanging out at one of the local pool halls the night before he was due to return to base from emergency leave to begin his discharge. Frankie Johnson came in, followed by his usual gang of deadbeats. Frankie was two years older than Billy, worked in the mill, and had a police record that dated back to age twelve. He was short but stockily built, with a bulldog face and a red, jagged scar under one eye. Frankie was a box-cutter man, kept one in his back pocket at all times, and was able to whip it out and slash before most people could throw a punch. Box-cutter wounds usually didn't kill, except in the neck, sliced about a half-inch deep and hurt.

On the east side, the unspoken rule was that if you were local you looked out for one another, or at least ignored each other if you weren't friends. For years, Frankie had built up his reputation until people left him alone; in return he left them alone if he knew them and they showed respect. He knew Billy. Knew he was Mike's son. Everyone knew Mike.

When Frankie came into the bar, the noise quieted in deference to his reputation while he inspected the crowd, decided everyone was cool and settled back to drink beer. Billy had his back to the door and was lining up a shot when Frankie passed. Frankie bumped the end of his cue and Billy cursed.

"Hey man, hey!" Frankie took hold of Billy's arm. "How 'bout showing a little respect for your elders?" He gave a little shove, stepped back and smiled. Normally Billy would have returned to his game, but Frankie's face was smug and sure.

"Yeah, well watch where you're going, umph?" Billy said.

"What where I'm going? Watch where I'm going!" Frankie gave his disciples an expression of mock surprise. "Skinhead said 'Watch where I'm going.'"

"It's not 'skinhead,' the name is Billy Riley."

"Oh, I'm sorry, Mr. Riley. I didn't mean to insult you," Frankie exclaimed again with wide eyes. There were mean grins on a lot of faces. A few people stepped back.

"Hey look, buddy," Frankie said suddenly and very seriously. "I know your old man just croaked and all, and maybe you're a little edgy. Happens to the best of us." Frankie pivoted slightly to one side, resting his hand on his hip pocket. Most of the eyes in the bar followed his hand. "You just tell me you're sorry, and we'll forget about the whole thing." Frankie looked into the faces that surrounded him and grinned. "Just a little 'I'm sorry,' and you're off the hook."

Billy's gaze followed Frankie's arm to where it disappeared behind his back. Even if he hadn't spent much time on the street, he knew the game.

"Wait one goddamn minute," Billy said, holding up one finger. "Give me just one goddamn second."

He stomped out of the bar towards Bubble's car. Everyone watched him leave, expecting him to drive away. Billy opened the door and reached under the seat. Then he straightened, one hand inside his shirt. When he came back in, he kept his hand in his shirt. There was a noticeable bulge.

"Now we can talk," he said, facing Frankie. "I ain't apologizing, and if you're wanting some shit, I have it now.

Again, Frankie grinned, but he was also licking his lips. The bartender picked up a phone.

"What you holding?" Frankie asked.

"Maybe what you're holding; maybe a whole lot more." He let the words sink in. The silence was like smoke. Billy kept it up, knowing he had the edge. "We're gonna fight. You know that. If you want, we can go clean, man to man. You throw down and I will."

"You go first," Frankie said.

Billy laughed. "I know damn well what you have, a box cutter. You don't know what I'm toting. You throw down and I will."

Frankie was still smiling, but one corner of his mouth twitched. His eyes moved from Billy's face to his shirt. Slowly, Frankie pulled his box cutter from his pocket and dropped it on the table. Billy smiled, then pulled a flashlight from out of his shirt.

"Joke," Billy said, as they came together. The fight ended in less than a minute, the gangling boy now hardened into a reckoning force and letting go totally for the first time in all his life. Frankie was carried away in an ambulance and Billy to jail.

Cotton Bain was next. Billy was jumped from behind and slashed across his back. The Bains and Johnsons stuck together. Billy had taken to carrying a knife, and he got a good swipe across Cotton's face before they dropped the weapons and went fist to fist. Billy knocked out most of Cotton's front teeth. Only the fact that Wallace pleaded self-defense got Billy out of jail.

The cut soldier in front of Jerry's drive-in solidified Billy's emergence as the newest bad ass east of the river. Younger boys began to imitate him and speak to him as he passed. Older people began to keep out of his way, especially when he was drinking. Billy had never asked for the title, nor wanted it, but his image grew daily.

10

A COLD autumn rain had begun to fall, so Bubble decided to take a break from building birdhouses. He had already sold ten of them through the pet shop and his profits were crying out to be spent. He paid a neighbor to drive to Willie's and pick up a case of wine and was later rocking and sipping on his front porch when Wilma came wobbling up to his gate. She stopped and lifted her hand, rain dripping off the wilted hat she wore.

"Bubble honey, can I come in?" she asked.

"Where's Punk?"

"He skipped out on me. I think the bastard's left town."

Bubble motioned her in with one hand. She carried a soaked pillowcase that bulged with odd shapes. She sat in a chair beside him, shivering, and wiped the water from her face.

"I hope the cocksucker's dead," Bubble said, feeling a twinge of pain flicker across his buttocks.

"He will be when I find him," Wilma swore. "Took every damn penny I had."

Bubble watched her shiver like a small gray dog that had crept on his porch. She brushed back her bangs, but they fell forward in long gray strands. She waved her knees back and forth.

"You need a drink?" Bubble lifted his fifth off the floor. Her arm jerked, as if her first impulse was to snatch the bottle away from him and get it into her mouth before he recanted. But she clenched her fist and held still.

"You got enough? I mean, I wouldn't want to take none if you're short."

Bubble handed her the bottle. She lifted it high and drank greedily, then stopped suddenly as if ashamed. She turned the bottle up again, then handed it to Bubble. Already she looked better, not so pale and shivering less.

"Where you been staying?" Bubble asked.

"Oh, around. Most everyone has left Willie's. Getting too cold." She looked hungrily at the bottle.

Bubble took a swallow, then passed it to her. "I guess you're wanting to stay here? That why you came by?"

Wilma hunched her shoulders and tried to look pitiful. "Could I, Bubble? For a little while? I could make things real nice for you here."

"I might not be here too much longer. This goddamn campaign of mine is costing me a bundle."

"I could get a job and help out—you know, at one of the diners." She leaned close, rubbing his arm. "Things could be real nice, us being here together."

Bubble grunted as he took the bottle back from her and set it on the floor. "Haven't you got anything dry? You need to get out of them wet clothes."

Wilma smiled sadly and slipped onto her knees. Without further words or ceremony, she unzipped Bubble's trousers and took him in her mouth, and committed herself to the agreement in the only way she knew.

WALLACE was parked outside the pet shop when Billy came out for lunch. He honked and motioned for Billy to get in.

"You revoking my bail or something?" Billy grinned as he shook Wallace's hand.

"And have you get out of working? Nope, I was just in the area. How's the pet business?"

"Boring."

"Not as boring as jail, I bet." Wallace tossed a paper sack into Billy's lap. "You like Arby's? I brought you a ham and cheese."

"Who doesn't like Arby's? What're you gonna eat?"

"Nothing. I'm on a diet."

"Yeah? So what really brings you out this way? Can't be just to give me a sandwich."

"I am your parole officer, you know."

"And I've been straight as a hoe handle. Just like I promised."

"I know. I talked with your boss the other day and he says you're doing fine. He even likes you."

Billy shrugged as he unwrapped his sandwich and took a bite.

"You thought anymore about what we were discussing last week?" Wallace asked.

"You mean school?" Billy mumbled with food in his mouth. "I thought about it for about an hour, then mostly forgot it."

"Forget it hell, Billy! What else you have in mind, working here the rest of your life?"

"I'm doing some thinking about things."

Wallace sighed. "Look Billy. You'd be a fool not to take advantage of this. VA will pay your way. Why, in four years time you can be anything you want."

"I don't see how school is going to help me. 'Sides, I'm not sure I'm the type to sit in a desk for four years."

"Would it mean anything to you if I told you Ruby is worried sick that you won't go?"

"Ruby worries about everything."

"She came by and asked me to say something to you. She'd like to see you get out of Fayetteville. I'd like to see you get out of here, too."

"Yeah? Well, college didn't do much for Bubble, did it? You seen him lately? He went for two years and now he's a pants-pissing wino."

"Bubble has problems, Billy. I don't know what they are, but he's always been weak. You, you're more like your dad was."

"I wouldn't say that."

"Well, you are, and you know, he wanted you to go to college really bad. I heard him say that often."

"He never told me. He never told me much of nothing."

"Well, he wanted you to go and I do and Ruby and Bubble, too. You owe it to yourself."

Billy finished his sandwich and crumpled the aluminun foil into a ball. He stared out the window. "Just give me some time to think, Wallace. I've only been out of the Corps for a few months. That's the only school I ever knew he wanted me in."

"O.K. All I ask is that you give it some thought. Hard thought. Son, it's just that the east side has a way of getting a hold on people and digging in deeper till they never can get away. Kinda like quicksand. I've seen it, in too many people."

"You got out."

"Yep, and it's only because I fought like hell. Like pure hell. I'd like to see it come a little easier for you."

"Like I said, I'll think it over."

Wallace started his car engine. "Hey, look. You care if I send in a few entrance applications for you? With those tests you took in the service, I think you could get in the spring semester. I know some people."

"Yeah, sure. Do what you like." Billy shook his hand and stepped from the car. As Wallace drove off, he stood and watched the car diminish to a speck.

FROM the mouth of a small creek flowing into the river, a breeze stirred the water, cool air that caused dandelion puffs to scurry before it. Billy sat with the canoe turned broadside to the current, slowly sliding down river. He liked the way the dandelion puffs raced like tiny cars, but silent, unlike the drone of traffic he still heard from the bridge up river. Evening was settling over the land, starting early beneath the willow and sweetgum that bowed over the river. Doves had begun their sad

cooing from the brush, and close to tangles in the water came
the puck of brim beginning to surface feed.

The canoe had belonged to Mike, but Billy could not remember once seeing his father in it. Chained to the base of an
oak in the back yard, it was always there when Bubble and Billy
went fishing, or for later when Billy had grown older and was
allowed to take the canoe out on his own.

The canoe spun until Billy could see down river. The shores
narrowed to a V, the higher tree branches streaked with colors
from the first frost of the year. A spot appeared against the
curtain of trees, lowering to the water as smoothly as the
dandelions sailed. The spot focused into a male mallard whose
feet skimmed the water before he sighted Billy, veered sharply
to the left and rose. Soon it was just a spot again.

You don't have to worry, fellow, Billy thought. I'm not
much on hunting.

Sighting the duck made him think again of a time when he
was very young. It was one of his earliest memories—a cold
morning with Mike and Bubble, standing on the stubble of a
cut wheat field. The men were dove hunting, his father dressed
in a bright, red coat, Bubble slender, wearing sun glasses that
glinted in the early morning glare. The doves were flying, and
already a pile of the birds lay at Billy's feet. He hated the roar
that jumped from the guns and made the birds fall; he had
learned to clamp his hands over his ears whenever the barrels
went up. Still, he could feel the blast, as if each time someone
placed their hand upon his chest and nudged him back. No
wonder the little birds fell, he had reasoned. Later in the morning he had begun to whimper because of the cold that had filled
his shoes and caused his feet to ache. His father had lifted him
and removed his shoes, placing his frigid feet inside his coat. His
feet soon stopped hurting, but holding to his father's neck, he
was unable to cover his ears whenever Bubble fired again. He
clung tightly, afraid the noise would make him fall like the
doves.

This evening was the first time he had been on the river in a couple of years, so Billy sat quietly, drinking in the silence and the coolness that hugged the water. He was glad there were no fishermen.

Same old river, Billy thought, same old place. I can't see where it's changed one inch since I was a kid; maybe that log floating over there is new but it looks the same as the one that floated by last time I was here. The water is still brown and the willow branches bend from the shore and brush the surface when the wind blows, and there are still water bugs spinning in the shallows that are sucked down by feeding brim, and ducks nest in the brush along shore, quack while leading you from their nests, and the doves, there have always been doves cooing from the forest; they sound so lonely.

Already high in the western sky sat a quarter moon, the cresent brilliant and silver against the sharp autumn twilight. The bottom half of the Sea of Tranquility was visible.

Seems like nature has a plan, Billy thought as he watched the moon. At least there is some permanence, cycles, happenings you can count on year after year. The Pleiades meteor shower will return every August, there will be no more leaves on the oak trees by mid November. Maybe the first robins will arrive in late February or mid March, but they will return. You can count on it.

Billy lifted a floating stick from the water, then slung it mid river. Humans just don't have a plan, do they? Billy wondered. Events or actions you can count on. Not in reality. Sure, we make plans, glorious plans, and set out to fulfill them, but winter may come in December or as early as September. Why should I plan? Astronomer, birdseed seller, bad ass, seems just as well to stumble along and let things surprise you.

Billy fastened the top button of his jacket against the chill. Dad thought he knew the plan, Billy thought. Bubble, he thinks now he has the answer. You'd think someone could make sense out of this shit. I don't know. Sometimes Ruby seems to know something I don't the way she always smiles, and then Cassie, looking into the distance as if she sees something just barely in sight.

Twilight was quickly filling the river. Billy reached for the paddle, then cut into the water, the splash especially loud. He looked over his shoulder, the channel slowly curving before rounding a bend. Ahead lay another bend.

River stays the same, Billy mused. Probably be the same a thousand years from now. Still, I always wonder what's coming around that next curve.

CASSIE had hoped Billy would be waiting when she came out at midnight, and he was, leaning against a lamp pole with his head tilted.

"What you see this time?" she asked. "Discovered a new planet?"

"No, but I think I've discovered a new star." Billy hugged her, lifting Cassie from the ground. "A bright, new green-eyed star."

Cassie smiled while planting a quick kiss on his cheek. "I'm hungry. Very hungry. What do you say we go to that diner again?"

"Suits me." They started up the street. Cassie seemed in good spirits to have danced all night. Billy listened to her hum low in her throat.

"You don't seem so tired tonight," Billy said.

"I've been working in that club one month tonight, Billy. One month, and I've saved over six hundred dollars."

"Hey, that's pretty good dough. Beats the hell out of selling birdseed."

Cassie twirled once, her hands arching over her head, ballerina style. "Maybe one more month, two at the most, and I'll have enough money to head for New York."

"Too bad you 'gotta keep working there. Now you have a little money, maybe you can find something besides dancing."

"Another month I can stand. Besides, where would I find another job that pays that kind of money?"

Billy shrugged. "You wouldn't. I just hate to think of you up there. Doesn't suit you."

"I'm *not* up there, Billy. At least in my mind. I imagine I'm in some place like Carnegie Hall, and all the drunk soldiers are rich people in fifty-dollar seats."

"And the beer is champagne, umph?" Billy asked.

"Yes. And the strobe light is really a spotlight and I'm doing a solo."

Billy chuckled. He thought back earlier in the evening when he had been on the river. He remembered how the river always curved ahead, and his smile faded.

Entering the restaurant, they took the same booth. The waitress recognized them and brought over two cups of coffee. Billy carefully sipped the hot coffee, often staring at the dark outside.

"What's on your mind?" Cassie asked later as they ate. "You seem distant."

"Distant? Naw." He shook his head. "Well, maybe I have a little something on my mind."

"You want to talk about it?"

"Not particularly, because I know what you'll say."

"You seem pretty sure of yourself for knowing me only a week."

Billy leaned over the table. "There's about a dozen people right now trying to make my mind up for me. You ever had that problem? Everyone has this big idea of what I should do."

"It must be nice having so many people who care. What's their idea?"

"That I go to school. Enter this next semester in one of the universities."

"Maybe you do know me. I think that's a wonderful idea."

"What would I do in college?"

"Anything you want. Study. Learn things. Become a spaceman."

"Do you think I could really go away and study astronomy?

I'm from the east side, girl. People here would laugh themselves
to death."

"Not the ones who count. I wouldn't worry about what the
others say."

"Well, I do." Billy drained his coffee and sopped his plate with
bread. "There's another thing, too," he said quietly.

"I'm listening."

Billy drummed his fingers against the table. "You're paying
way too much for that rinky-dink room of yours."

"It's cheap. I need to live cheaply."

"Yeah. I think maybe I can help you out. I have this apartment
rented, see. Nothing fancy, but it's large and just over the
bridge. Not in the rough section. What you think about moving
in?"

Cassie wrinkled her brow, then stared at her plate.

"Hey, I know you're into this reality stuff," Billy said quickly.
"No commitments. No problem here. You'll just be my roommate." Billy whispered. "My fucking roommate."

Cassie tried not to smile. "You seem mighty damn sure of
yourself, Mr. Riley. What makes you think last night was the
start of something?"

"I never said it was. I'm just making you a business offer. You
keep an eye on the place while I'm at work, and nights you have
a free place to sleep. Simple as that."

"I don't think I've ever been hustled quite this way."

"Who's hustling!"

She was smiling now. "I'll have to think about it."

"Take your time. Think about it while we walk over and
check the place out."

The walk was brisk, the air cold and invigorating. Cassie
dumped a handful of dry leaves down Billy's shirt. He chased
her across someone's lawn, then barked back so fiercely at a
collie watchdog that the dog retreated. Coming off the bridge
ramp into the east side, they walked hand in hand. Billy never
noticed the jacked-up Chevy parked by the corner, or the
soldier watching so intently from inside.

BILLY decided it was the clock he hated most about the psychiatrist's office. In the silence between words, it ticked loudly and consistently, as if measuring and graphing this hour of his life. He wished he could sling it through the window, and let in more light. The doctor sat upright at his desk, hands folded, waiting for Billy to finish his sentence.

"Yeah, it was a white rat, not a wharf rat. One of those albino types that my uncle bought me from a pet store."

"And the rat bit you. Badly?"

"Naw, not bad, but it hurt like hell. Drew a little blood."

"And you didn't kill it?"

"Like I said, I started to. Had my air rifle in my hands and was considering popping him behind the head. Then I noticed this silk scarf of Ruby's hanging on the clothesline and had another idea."

The doctor nodded, then propped his chin on one hand. Billy stopped talking and cleared his throat. "You want to hear this, really? It's sort of a dumb story."

"Sure. I'm certain it's no dumber than many other things people do."

"Yeah, well, I'll tell it since you seem to have this fascination about how I feel about rats." Billy swallowed, then continued the story. "So, when I saw the scarf, I had this bright idea to make a parachute for the rat. Not shoot him, but sort of mess with his head a little bit. I found some mason twine and tied pieces of it to the corners of the scarf, then knotted the ends and looped them around the rat's belly. Then, I rolled up the scarf and wound the strings around the outside and tucked the bundle in close."

"How was the rat behaving?"

"Not too bad. Sort of scared I guess, wondering what was going on. Well, I leaned back, and slung that rat as high in the air as I could. You should have seen it. Soon as he started coming down, the chute unfurled just perfect and blossomed out, and the rat was floating real slow with his feet sticking straight out and his eyes busting out of his head. A couple of turds popped out of him like bombs. I was laughing myself silly."

The doctor nodded, then smiled.

Billy stopped his story and pointed at the window blinds. "Why don't you open up the shade and let some air in here? Why you keep this place so gloomy?"

"Most people prefer the room dark. They say it's relaxing."

"Not me. I say it's depressing."

When the doctor turned and opened the shades, sunlight fell across the desk. Billy stared at the dust floating in it. He squinted, then resumed his story. "Well, the rat was O.K. Good as new. Landed like he was lying on a pillow. I picked him up, looked him over and he was fine except for his heart thumping like mad. I decided we were even then, that I'd let him go. Then, I got to thinking about all the bread and corn I'd fed him over the past week and decided I ought to sling him up one more time. Kinda like paying his debt to society."

"And it was fun, too. Wasn't it?" the doctor asked.

"Yeah, sure it was fun. Didn't you ever pick on animals when you were a kid?"

"I did, and pulled a few stunts meaner than what you're telling me."

Billy looked again into the shaft of light. "So I fixed up the parachute once more and slung the rat up, and down he came floating just as easy as the first time. It was funny; you could see how scared he was. Then I sent him up again, one for his country. He did great, so I let him rest a while and awarded him some scraps of bread. Like giving him a medal, that sort of thing, duty above and beyond. A meritorious rat."

Billy licked his lips and lowered his voice. "Then I decided to take him one step further, this being an award-winning rat, an above-average rat. One more time, I said to the rat, and you'll come smack down on top of the American dream, and you'll go straight to the woods to retire. So I pitched him up again for the last time and when he reached the top, what you call it, the zenith, and started to tumble down, he got tangled up in the strings and the chute wouldn't open, and he fell the whole rest of the way, flat on top of a rock surrounding one of my aunt's flower beds."

Billy stopped, stared into the light again, then back at the doctor. "I tried to catch him, but he slipped right through my hands, hit once, bounced and that was it. Deader than hell."

Slowly, the doctor nodded. Billy studied an amber paper-weight with an encased fly, then grinned. "You wanted a rat story, Doc. I told you one. You're sure I'm crazy now, huh?"

"I've never thought you were crazy, Billy."

Billy reared back in his chair and laughed. "So, what the hell, want a moral to this, Doc? If you're a rat, don't take up flying. Don't try to imitate a bird or a paratrooper. And for God's sake, don't let them keep throwing you up. Bite, kick, scratch and scream."

The doctor began tapping his temple with a pencil eraser. Billy picked up the paper weight. "You should have stayed away from that last turd, fly."

"Do you think a lot of people act like rats?" the doctor asked. "You said that earlier."

"The dumb ones do."

"And who are they?"

"The people who keep hanging on to the strings. Up again and up again and up again, you know? It's all the same until you try to make it down safely again one last time."

AFTER Cassie moved her stuff over, even her few possessions made the apartment look homier. Billy spent two hours scrubbing the floors with Lysol and bought new sheets for the bed. Cassie hung her posters and cleaned the bathroom with Ajax and steel wool. They were settled and comfortable by the end of the week.

Saturday, Billy invited Bubble and Ruby for dinner so they could meet Cassie. Bubble was sober enough to crack jokes and flirt with Cassie, and Ruby seemed cordial, though Billy knew she didn't like him living with a topless dancer. Billy was light-hearted, slightly drunk, flipping hamburgers with a spatula and wearing a grocery bag as a chef's hat.

After dinner, they sat in the living room and talked while eating a half gallon of Breyer's chocolate fudge ice cream. Then Ruby led Cassie into the kitchen to do the dishes.

"Nice gal," Bubble said after they had gone. "Kinda strange, but damn good looking."

"She wants to be a dancer."

"I thought she's a dancer now?"

"She wants to be a ballerina or something. Wants to dance on Broadway in Carnegie Hall."

"Carnegie Hall ain't on Broadway."

"Well, one of those places. You know what I mean."

Bubble rattled his empty beer can and looked to see where Ruby was. "She sounds like a girl with ambition. I can't say the same for you."

Billy flopped back in his chair. "Ruby's been talking to you, too? She might as well take an ad out in the paper."

"Boy, it would sure beat selling them damn fish and dogs. You'd come out of college with a degree, and with the money Mike left you, you'd be set up."

"I could take that money right now and buy me a Cad and hustle up a few women and have a fortune in two years. I bet I'd look good in one of them broad-brimmed nigger hats."

"You don't take nothing serious no more, do ya?" Bubble asked. "You used to be a right serious kid."

Billy frowned and headed for the kitchen. "Hey, bring me one," Bubble hissed.

At the sink, the two women stopped talking. "Don't bring him one!" Ruby ordered. "Lord, he's had enough already."

Billy carried the last of the six-pack into the living room.

"Ruby said you can't have no more," he said and grinned. Billy opened a can, tilted back his head, and poured a stream of lager into his mouth. Bubble watched for a moment, then grabbed a can.

"To hell with Ruby," he said.

Billy dropped into his chair. He tried balancing his can on one knee. "I hear you're living with some whore these days. One of them wino ladies."

"I wouldn't go so far as to call her a whore."

"I wouldn't call her a Sunday school teacher, either," Billy said. "I even heard she's the ole lady of that guy who cut you."

Bubble grunted. "She's down on her luck. I'm just letting her hang around for a while."

"You should have brought her tonight."

"Naw. She was drunk. Drinks more than I do."

After several minutes, the ladies came from the kitchen. Ruby glared at the can in Bubble's hand while putting on her coat. Bubble quickly downed the can.

"Billy, honey, we sure thank you for the nice supper and for letting us meet Cassie," Ruby said.

Bubble nodded. "You'll come fishing, won't you? You and Cassie both."

"Wouldn't miss it," Billy said.

Ruby hugged their necks. "If he gives you any trouble," Ruby said, "you just come and tell me. I'll take a stick to him."

Cassie smiled as they left, closing the door softly.

"So, that wasn't too bad, was it?" Billy asked. "They liked you."

"Ruby didn't at first. I guess she was expecting me to come out wearing a G-string."

"Ah, don't worry about Ruby. She just has to get used to new things. She practically raised me, you know."

"After I talked to her about why I'm dancing here, she seemed to warm up. We talked a lot while washing the dishes."

Billy rolled his eyes. "I can imagine about what. She wants

you to persuade me to go to school, right? That's all that's on her mind these days."

"She loves you Billy."

"Yeah, she loves me all right. It's just that she loves with the power of a Mack diesel."

11

CASSIE liked weekend nights better. The bar was full then, a sea of faces stretching from wall to wall that blended together into a collage of staring eyes and gaping mouths. That was better than the slow nights when the eyes in a single face hunching forward over a beer mug, tracked her movements on the stage. She had trouble then keeping her mind where it had to be if she was to survive this job—far beyond the bar, in the city of her dreams, under bright lights on a popular stage. There she spun and leaped to music that swelled from the orchestra pit, violins and brass horns and silver-toned strings. There she was Peter Pan and the audience loved her.

Single faces had a way of prying into her mind, as if thought waves were stronger when not mixed together. She would look into a stranger's face for a moment and it would frighten her. The illusion was broken momentarily. She would think: the air stinks, smells of old beer and cigarettes, the walls are grotesque, painted with fat and skinny nude dancing women. The music is too loud. Always, before she could tear her eyes away from the face, the man would smile, maybe wink. She knew what he was thinking. Hell of a place to be working, girl.

She remembered the day she arrived in town. Raining, forgetting her umbrella in her haste to leave the car where the man tried to feel her up. The clouds were low and gray over the streets, and she wandered numbly, occasionally touching the five-dollar bill in her shirt. Her heart had leaped when she spied the sign over the doorway, DANCERS NEEDED NOW.

She was inside the bar before she realized what kind of dancers were needed. Still, she asked for the manager, a stocky, cigar-smoking man with greasy hair. He led her to a back room.

"Yeah, I need some dancers," he said, staring her up and down. "You done it before?"

"Only ballet."

He laughed. "Sister, I don't care how you dance, as long as your tits are bouncing."

Cassie surprised herself by nodding.

"Yeah, well I gotta see your hardware first," he said.

Cassie's mind was already shifting gears, lifting her until the man and tiny room shrank. She slowly unbuttoned her shirt and removed it, then her bra. The man nodded, thrusting out his bottom lip. When he quickly brushed one of her nipples, Cassie didn't slap him, only lifted her chin an inch higher, reducing the man an inch lower.

"You don't have the clap, do you?"

"No."

"No messing around with the customers while working. What you line up on the side is your business. Pay is two hundred a week and you keep your tips. Can you start tonight?"

Cassie nodded, then turned around and began dressing. She had always had this ability to tune out unpleasant happenings. She first learned to close off her mind to the surrounding world in grammar school. She was always the new kid in class. During one stretch, she moved through five foster homes in only four years. All the stares, the whispers—orphan girl—she discovered she could stare when talking to someone at the bridge of their nose. That way, she could avoid their eyes. Eyes were the only part of a person that couldn't lie. I don't want to know your secrets, Cassie used as her motto, because I'm just passing through, then moving on.

Tonight was Friday, and the bar was packed, the sea of faces surrounding her, fused together into an off-color, slowly spinning carousel. No single faces, single eyes, only a wall surrounding her. She felt safe—don't tell me your secrets. Billy. Sweet, sweet Billy. Nicest person I've met in a long time. But those eyes, they crackle with emotion all the time. Poor Billy, she thought sadly. Emotions will be his downfall yet.

THEY went fishing the next morning, a fine fall day with the leaves in full change. The weather was crystal and warm—Indian summer—as if the sun was shedding the last of its energy before winter. For years, Bubble had fished where Lewis Creek flowed into the river. He kept the weeds chopped back so that brown grass now covered the small clearing. The creek had formed a sandbar, its edge dropping steeply into deep water where fish fed.

Wilma came, wearing a lacy black Sunday dress she had pulled from a Salvation Army clothes dump, with a pair of old, still-white Converse hightops. She looked ridiculous, but the dress was clean and pressed, her hair combed, and she followed Bubble with short, bouncy steps. Cassie was carrying a picnic basket filled with fried chicken and deviled eggs and potato salad. Upon his head Bubble balanced a cooler full of beer and wine. Billy brought up the rear, toting the fishing gear and a portable tape player. They wound down the path between great oaks and sweetgums, tramping through ankle-deep red and gold leaves.

In the clearing above the sandbar, the sun shone brightly. They spread two blankets. Cassie placed the picnic basket on top of a boulder, away from marauding troops of ants, while Billy slid an Emmy Lou Harris tape into the player.

"Like paradise, ain't it?" Bubble asked. He sat on his blanket and untied his shoes. "How 'bout throwing your uncle a beer?" he called to Billy. He tossed his shoes towards the rock. "Good as paradise."

Billy pitched him a beer, then another when he saw Wilma staring hungrily. Cassie took great care in fixing their blanket,

removing small sticks and pebbles from underneath, then flat-
tening out the wrinkles. When she finished, the blanket was
taut as canvas. She settled slowly, folding her legs underneath
her.

Billy stood facing the water, smelling the breeze, a good
mixture of fish and warm water and rotting leaves along shore.
The current moved so slowly, that he only realized it moved
at all by sticks drifting past.

"Close to paradise, anyway," Billy answered Bubble. "I'd take
it over playing a harp." He stood watching until Cassie called
him to come sit down.

Cassie rolled back on the blanket, her long hair fanning and
framing her face. She smiled into the sunlight that lit up her
features.

"It is nice," she whispered to Billy. "We should have come
here before."

Billy peeled off his shirt to use for a pillow.

"Is it O.K. if I do that?" Cassie asked. "Take off my shirt? I
have a bra on."

Billy shrugged. "Hey Bubble," he called. "You gonna have
a heart attack if Cassie takes off her shirt?"

"I'm *wearing* a bra, Billy," she said in defense.

"Honey," Bubble answered. "A tit is a tit."

"I just want to get some sun. There may not be another chance
this year." She unbuttoned her flannel shirt and took it off,
folding the garment carefully. She was wearing a stretch bra,
and as her nipples hardened against the chill they pushed the
fabric. Bubble smiled and settled back.

Wilma watched for a moment; then as if knowing nothing
more than to mimic others, she slid her loose dress down both
shoulders. With her sagging breasts lost in an old French bra a
size too big, she was no competition for Cassie, but she smiled
at her boldness and glanced toward Bubble for his approval.
Bubble grunted and draped one arm across her bare shoulders.

"God help us," Billy whispered, caught between slight disgust and amusement. He turned his back and busied himself opening a beer. As he swallowed, the beer felt especially cold with the sun on his face.

"You think we ought to set some lines," Billy asked. "The sun is getting up pretty high."

"After this beer," Bubble answered. "Plenty of time yet."

Long ago, Billy had realized that fishing for Bubble was a sideline for drinking. Bubble never cared if he caught any fish or not, just enjoyed sitting back sipping on a beer, watching the red-and-white bobbers perk up and down. The fish weren't very important to Billy, either; the sun and the water brought him here. But having a hook in the water soothed the guilt from hearing his father say over and over—idle time is wasted time.

Billy opened the fishing case and lifted out three brim busters and a can of night crawlers. He began sliding out the sections of the rods. Bubble tossed his can into a growing pile of empties and reached for another.

"You going to get drunk if you keep that up," Billy warned. "I don't want to have to tote your drunk butt home."

"You just worry about hooking them worms right," Bubble answered. "I'll worry about the state of my drunkenness."

They left the women lying happily in the sun and went on the sandbar to set their poles. Billy jammed the butts deep in the sand while Bubble tossed the lines into the current. The lines were weighted with large sinkers but still the water pulled the lines until taut.

"Think we'll catch anything?" Cassie asked, strolling out onto the sand. "Can you believe I've never been fishing!"

"We'll catch something, all right," Bubble answered. "Maybe no more than a case of chiggers, but we'll carry something home."

Cassie sat on a log that had washed against the bank. "You want some of this?" She held up a joint of marijuana toward Billy. "You like to smoke pot?"

Billy gawked at the smoke curling around her fingers. "I thought you didn't do that kind of stuff. You don't even drink beer!"

"I only smoke once in a while. When I'm doing something especially nice. You don't smoke pot?"

"Sure. Once in a while." He took the joint and looked it over. "Where'd you get it?"

"From one of the girls. Don't worry, it's O.K."

Billy raised the joint and sucked down a long draw, then slowly exhaled in a steady blue stream. Bubble walked over.

"Want to try a new thing?" Billy asked him. "You ever tried any reefer?"

Bubble stared at the marijuana as if at a snake.

"That shit'll make you crazy."

"It won't make *you* crazy. You're already crazy." Billy took another draw, then he returned the joint to Cassie.

"Try it, Bubble," she said. "It'll make you feel good."

Bubble pinched the joint between his fingers and inspected it carefully, sniffing the sweet smoke.

"Try it," Billy urged. "It's not nearly as bad as that rot-gut wine you drink."

Bubble inhaled deeply, coughed, then took another puff. He flicked ashes from the end while exhaling, then squinted one eye. "Ain't shit to this stuff. I ain't seeing no colors yet." Cassie giggled. "I thought it was supposed to knock off the top of your head." He handed the joint to Cassie and slowly climbed the bank to the clearing.

Billy sat with Cassie on the log and finished the joint, a floating intoxication coming over him in warm buzzing waves. The colors of the river and trees seemed to mute and soften without distinct definition. A bobolink called from the trees, and the notes were sharp and bell-like. Billy liked the feeling on such a fine day and sat in silence holding Cassie's hand, watching the water slip by.

"Take a walk?" Cassie finally asked.

"Yeah, sure. Let me get a beer first." Billy took long, slow steps up the bank to the cooler. He fished a beer from the ice.

"Ain't shit to that stuff," Bubble muttered again from the blanket where he and Wilma were into a jug of wine.

They walked down a fisherman's path for about a hundred yards to a small mossy space beneath a huge old oak. Cassie suddenly twirled then fell back on the moss.

"This is wonderful, Billy. I've never felt so free and good!"

"It's the dope."

"No it's not. It's this day; it's living. Something out here makes me very happy."

Billy sat beside her. "I always liked the river. Me and Bubble used to come here often when I was little."

"Did you come with your dad, too?"

"Naw, maybe once or twice. He wasn't much on fishing and stuff." Billy took a swig from his beer. "Sure got the cotton mouth," he said.

Cassie leaned against him, gazing overhead into the branches. "I feel like I'm dancing. That's it. I feel good, the way I feel when I'm dancing ballet." She traced her finger slowly up his arm. "How do you feel?"

"O.K. Sort of high."

"But good?"

"Yeah, good. He stared over her shoulder at the curve of her breast under the bra. "Maybe just a little horny."

"Good," Cassie said and turned, cupping her hands behind his head.

BUBBLE and Wilma hit their jug of wine hard. The bright sun and the grass he sat in reminded Bubble of Willie's back lot and his pledge for Billy. Wilma was simply happy to drink no matter the reason, so they passed the bottle back and forth regularly, laying the foundation for a good drunk. When the

Emmy Lou tape ended, Bubble slid in his own tape, a collection
of Mozart classics. He turned the volume lower and leaned on
one elbow with a look of great satisfaction.

"Why you like that stuff?" Wilma asked. "I never knew
anyone who listened to that kind of stuff."

"That's 'cause you never hung around with anyone with class.
I been liking Mozart since I took a music appreciation class back
in school."

"I heard you were a college man once. Why'd you stop? You
might be a doctor or something big if you'd stayed."

Bubble took a long glug-glug-glug from the bottle. "Got a
bait of learning. Wasn't much to it, anyway."

Bubble stood and shaded his eyes with one hand. The glare
off the water was bright, and even squinting his eyes he couldn't
see the corks. His legs wobbled from the wine, so he closed his
eyes for a moment.

"Gonna check the lines," he said. He started down the bank,
slipped and slid several yards on his behind, cursed, and made
the sandbar. The lines were empty, the bait nibbled away.
Bubble rebaited the hooks and threw them back.

When ripples fanned from where the last line struck the
water, Mike's face appeared in them, jumping and shimmering
but staring with intensity into Bubble's face.

"Why'd you lie?" Mike asked. "You told a lie to that
woman."

"I wasn't lying, and you're dead."

"Maybe I'm dead, but you lied. Why don't you just tell her
you didn't have the balls to stay in school?"

Bubble stooped and picked up a stone. "You can't come
here," he shouted. "You can't come where you never came
before." He heaved the rock into Mike's face. The water
jumped. "It ain't right for you to mess with me here."

The water quieted and reflected just the sky and clouds.
Bubble stared at the reflection while sweat beaded on his forehead. Then he stumbled back up the hill.

"Who were you talking to?" Wilma asked. "I heard you talking."

"Just someone on the river. Someone in a boat." Bubble sat down heavily and reached for the bottle.

AFTERWARDS, Billy and Cassie lay on their backs and watched clouds passing through the branches.

I never did it before when I was high," Billy said. "Strange feeling, you know?"

"A good feeling," Cassie said.

The moss was littered with acorns and Billy began to feel them stabbing his back. He sat up and reached for his jeans.

"Don't get dressed yet," Cassie said. "Lay here for a while."

"Damn acorns are poking in my back." He folded his trousers for a cushion. Cassie folded her legs Indian style.

"Some hunter come along and he'll think we're crazy," Billy said.

"No, he won't. He'll probably just get behind a tree and watch."

Billy gave the forest a quick sweep with his eyes. He slung a handful of acorns into the water.

"Plenty of acorns. Must be a hard winter coming."

"Isn't this a wonderful tree?" Cassie said. "I bet we couldn't circle the trunk with both our hands together." Her eyes followed the trunk skyward. "I think it's grand how nature can take something as tiny as an acorn and make it grow into a tree this size."

Billy picked up another handful of acorns and let them sift through his fingers. "I think it's a little unfair, too," he said. "Look at how many acorns there are on the ground."

"What's unfair about that?"

"They can't all grow into big trees. Maybe just one in a million."

"Well, if they all grew into giants, there wouldn't be room for nothing else in the world."

"Yeah, still, what about all the ones that don't make it? Wouldn't you think that all acorns are created equal?"

"You're silly."

"No, listen. Why's it just got to be that one in a million that makes a big tree? All those acorns falling to the ground looking just alike, and all wanting to grow into some huge oak beside the river, and nearly every one will rot or be eaten by a squirrel, or if they're real lucky maybe grow into a sapling until a fire comes along or someone with a chain saw."

"That's nature, baby. The strong survive."

Billy felt his can of beer. It was warm, but he drank anyway. He took another acorn and flicked it into the air. "I don't know if the strong survive, or just hope and hurt the longest. It's mostly damn good luck that determines if you make it. Like the acorn that falls and bounces into soft, wet mud and then along comes a racoon or deer and shits right beside it. All the benefits, but damn good luck."

Cassie dug out a plug of moss and held it against the sky where she could see the spore pods. When she thumped it, spores fell in a yellow rain. "Look at it this way, Billy. The moss and the acorns and people, they're all the same." She clasped her hands around her knees. "Let's imagine that this big old oak is a family. It has a plan. Let's call it the acorn plan. Sure, there's lots of members of the family who strike out, whatever, get burned, eaten, maybe make it halfway only to get cut down. Still, this family knows that sooner or later one of them is going to fall on rich soil—maybe there is a little luck needed—but that person will grow and grow and grow. See?"

"Yeah, I see. Still doesn't seem fair."

"It isn't exactly fair." She flipped a handful of acorns over her head. "No, it's not exactly fair, Billy. Nothing is. But doesn't it make you feel good to know that one of these little acorns is one day going to be a hundred feet high? And it'll produce a million more acorns and eventually another tree will follow."

Cassie thrust her chin so high, Billy couldn't help smiling. "You've smoked too much of that dope."

"Then give me more if it makes me think this clearly. Billy, you have to understand. I'm the lucky acorn. The one who is going to make it." She swelled out her chest and her breasts rose and looked very white.

"It's hard to take a naked lady serious," Billy said. "Why don't you put on some clothes?"

"Ugh!" she cried. "You! Billy, I don't need any clothes today. Give me something I need."

"What do you need?"

"That's for you to decide. It's a game, dummy. Give me something you think I need."

Billy rubbed his chin, then leaned and kissed her nose. "I give you a kiss."

Cassie then kissed both his cheeks. "I give you a million kisses while we sit in a bathtub of bubbling champagne."

There was a small stone lying on the moss, a chunk of granite with quartz running through the middle. Billy held it to the light. "I give you a diamond."

Cassie found her own pebble. "I give you a diamond-covered beer mug." Her eyes sparkled and Billy thought he was beginning to understand the game. He galloped his hand across the moss.

"I give you a horse that just won the Triple Crown."

She caught his fingers. "I make you the jockey of that horse that just won the Triple Crown."

"I give you a telescope that can see all the planets."

"I give you the stars and planets."

"You're cheating," Billy exclaimed. "It's not possible to give the things you say."

"I not only give you the stars and planets, but a hamster that sings 'Ave Maria,' and a can of beer that never runs out."

"I don't understand." Billy frowned, beginning to not like the game.

Cassie placed her fingers against his temples. "Think! I asked you to give me something I need. What do I need most?"

"A thousand nights on Broadway."

"There you go, baby," she said. "But don't you see, you can't give me that. I can only do it for myself."

"Well, what about all that diamond mug and stars crap? You can't give that to me, either."

"Yes, I can. It's no further away than your imagination. What I can't give you is the thing you need inside to grow as big as that oak tree. Even you don't know what that is yet."

Billy flipped his can into the water. He began to pull on his clothes. "Get dressed. It's time to eat."

"I make you mad?"

"No. I'm hungry." All the way back to the clearing, her words buzzed in his head.

They found Bubble and Wilma roaring drunk. They had emptied one bottle and started the second, forgetting paper cups and drinking straight from the bottle. Fish were on both lines, but Bubble sat dumbly watching the lines slice through the water. Billy reeled in the fish and dropped them into a bucket.

"You're drunk as hell," he said, looking down on Bubble. "Here it is barely past noon and you're so wasted you can't stand up."

"I can stand up if I wanna. Can't I Wilma?" She nodded. "I stood up to fetch this last bottle."

Wilma was quickly settling into a stupor and, as Billy watched, she rocked backwards and sprawled across the blanket, eyes closed.

"You eaten anything?" Billy asked. "You better eat something fast."

"Don't want nothing," Bubble mumbled, " 'cept more wine." He tipped up the bottle. Billy toted over the picnic basket.

"Here, eat this." He handed Bubble a chicken leg. Bubble took the drumstick and looked at it, then dropped it on the blanket.

"You eat that chicken, or I'm going to cram it down your throat," Billy said.

Bubble licked his bottom lip, then turned up the bottle again.

Then he picked up the chicken and tossed it onto the sandbar. He tried to stand, but his legs buckled and he went down.

"You help me up from here, boy, and I'll stomp your ass." He made another attempt to stand, but Billy stuck his foot out and pushed him down. Cassie grabbed Billy's arm.

"A bad ass, ain't you?" Bubble said. "Here I'm dying for ya, and you're gonna cram a chicken leg down my throat."

"Why you have to drink like this? You're killing yourself."

"I'm dying for ya, hear me? You cutthroat son of a bitch. Help me up from here."

"Your dying ain't going to help me," Billy said while Cassie pulled at his arm. "That's crazy talk." Bubble leaned for the bottle, turned it over, and spilled a cup full or more on the blanket. Finally, he got the bottle to his mouth and drank loudly.

"I'm dying for ya, hear? You better yet? You through cutting people?"

Cassie pulled Billy down the bank. "Leave him awhile. He's just drunk." Billy picked up a handful of sand and slung it into the river.

"You any better yet?" Bubble hollered. "You gonna have to get better fast."

Billy flopped down in the sand and watched ants swarm over the drumstick. Bubble shouted several more times.

"He's passed out," Billy said after the shouting stopped.

"Why does he drink so much, Billy? He seems so intelligent sometimes."

"I don't know," Billy answered, "but he's getting worse. He keeps drinking at this rate, he won't make it till Christmas."

"It just doesn't make sense," she said. "He even listens to Mozart."

Billy kicked sand over the chicken. "I guess he's just one of the bad acorns," he said, giving Cassie a sidelong glance.

They finished the picnic on the sandbar and pulled in five more catfish. By late afternoon, Bubble and Wilma had sobered

enough to walk. A cold front moving in from the west was
bringing clouds and a stiff, cold wind. As the others moved up
the path, Billy stood on the bank and looked over the darkening
waters with an uncomfortable feeling he was seeing the fishing
bank for the last time.

12

OCTOBER slid into November, and the leaves fell in colorful showers after the heavy frosts began. Billy continued to work in the pet store, and Cassie danced, and Bubble built birdhouses, and Ruby waited tables, collecting the dollar bills left beside yolk-splattered plates. The days took on that crisp, clear fall look when the heat and moisture leave the air, and the sharp cold starts in your nose when you breathe in deeply just after sunset.

Often, Billy waited outside the bar for Cassie, and they would go to the diner or walk the dark streets to the east side, kicking piles of leaves and breathing silver clouds of vapor. Cassie saved four hundred dollars the second month, hid it in an old shoe in the closet, and talked of going north soon.

"You just might make it," Billy said one night as they walked. "I wouldn't have bet a nickle on you when we first met, but now, you just might."

"I *will* make it," she answered. "Dancing is the only thing that matters."

For a moment, Billy wished she would lie, say he mattered. They had learned one another's ways. Nights were warm and good together, though he still awoke each morning and turned to see if she was there. She was truthful; he would always come second to her dancing. He had to admit that truth was better than living with lies.

Bubble drank even heavier after the fishing trip. He stretched his small income by drinking only the cheapest wine. Wilma waited tables for a week, paid the light bill and bought some groceries, then was fired for coming to work drunk. Billy stopped by often, but found he and Bubble could not be together long without arguing over college and drinking.

Billy received his first acceptance letter to school just before Thanksgiving. He stared at the return address of the university, surprised that Wallace had actually applied for him. He stuffed the envelope in his back pocket, and later, at work, tried to busy himself and forget it had arrived. Often, he would stop and feel its bulk and wonder what it said. Finally, during lunch he gave in. He slit the end of the envelope and slid out the letter and began to read.

"What do you know about that!" he whispered and tried to force down his smile. "Accepted at Carolina."

Billy carefully folded the letter and put it into his pocket. He sat staring at the ground in disbelief, opening the letter several times to read it again.

After work he wandered the checkerboard of alleys and narrow streets in front of the mill. Several younger boys followed him at a respectful distance, but Billy was so deep in thought he hardly noticed them. He was surprised to find himself standing in front of Ruby's house. A light shone through the curtain, so he knocked. Soon, he heard Ruby's footsteps.

"You busy or something?" he asked when Ruby opened the door. "I can come back later if you're busy."

"Lord, no!" She gave him a big hug. "You come in out of that cold."

Billy glanced around the room. There were no cigarette butts or men's clothes visible.

"I was just walking around and thought I'd stop by for a minute. You doing O.K.?"

"I'm doing, same as always." She directed him toward a chair. "You hungry? There's some pork chops I can fry up."

"No. I like to wait and eat with Cassie."

"Not just a bite? That's a long time to wait. Here, I'll get you some coffee. Your hands are cold as ice."

She hurried to the stove. Billy knew there was no use arguing with Ruby when food was involved. She was back soon with a steaming cup and slice of chocolate pie.

"I thought you'd probably be working," Billy said.

"No, I'm back on days now. Don't work nights again till next week."

"How's your friend doing. Harold I think's his name."

Ruby busied herself sitting carefully and arranging the hem of her skirt. "He's all right. I see him when he has a load coming through."

Billy sipped his coffee, feeling the thick letter in his pocket.

"What's on your mind, honey?" Ruby asked. "You seem to have something on your mind."

Billy hesitated a moment before pulling the letter from his pocket. "Take a look at this."

At first, Ruby handled the letter as if it was hot. She read the return address. "Gracious, I was scared it was from the court house. What is this?" She quickly opened the envelope and read the first lines aloud. Then she smiled and flopped against the back of the couch. "Billy," she squealed. She rose and hugged him again. "I'm so proud, I don't know what to say."

"It doesn't mean nothing." He tried to sound gruff. "It doesn't mean I'm going to go."

"Of course you'll go. You have to go. Honey, no person in their right mind would pass up an opportunity like this."

She finished reading the letter. "University of North Carolina, even. That's where Wallace went to school."

"Yeah, and don't let on that you didn't put Wallace up to this. He sent in the application, you know."

"Well, I just told him how much I wished you would go. That's all."

"Well, don't get too worked up yet. I'm not sure what I'll do." He sloshed coffee around in his mouth before swallowing. "I have to admit, it feels good. I never would have thought that Carolina would accept me."

"You say the craziest things, Billy. Why wouldn't they? You forgotten all those good grades you used to get. You hardly ever got a 'C.' "

Billy finished his coffee and stood to go. Ruby tried to give him a chicken salad sandwich. She followed him to the door.

"You and Cassie come over and eat. You never come over."

"We will, Ruby."

"And Billy," she said, catching his arm, "I'm so proud of you."

"Well, like I said. I haven't made up my mind yet."

"Just think about it, umph? Do that for me."

Billy hurried down the steps and into the night. Ruby sang while washing out his coffee cup.

CASSIE was so thrilled over his acceptance letter that instead of going to the diner, she insisted they take a cab to a steak house across town. She ordered a bottle of champagne and toasted him above the flickering lights of a candle.

"To the next great brain of the world. May science never be the same."

"This is silly. I doubt I even go."

"You'll go. If Ruby and I have to tie you limb to limb and mail you, you'll go."

They ordered thick steaks, baked potatoes and fresh salad, then laughed over which fork went with which course of food. Finally, they decided to stay with the same fork, reasoning that some poor person would be washing dishes long after they had gone.

"I guess it makes me feel sort of guilty," Billy said as they ate, "to even consider going to school for four years."

"I don't understand."

"Well, take Ruby," he said. "Woman's worked like a dog all her life trying to have something and look after me and Bubble on the side. Here, I'm thinking of going off to college, drink beer and chase coeds, and she's still gonna be right there hustling them blue-plate specials and hoping one day to land a man. It doesn't seem fair."

"Who ever said the world was fair?"

"Yeah, well I don't like adding to the unfairness."

"Billy, you know there's nothing in the world that would make Ruby happier than seeing you make a big shot of yourself."

"Maybe so, but it seems that the people who deserve the breaks never get them."

"And the acorns fall and fall. Remember?"

"I'm not talking about no damn acorns, Cassie. I'm talking about people—good people. People who sweat and fart and cry. You've never heard Ruby crying in her bedroom because some SOB trucker left her high and dry."

"Maybe she sets herself up for that."

"Yeah, I agree. Sometimes she does. But you'd think that sooner or later with all those goddamn acorns bouncing around, a good one would bump into her."

"You're making fun of me."

"Who's making fun?" Billy pushed his salad aside. "My old man fought in the war. Deader than hell at fifty-five. Ruby's crying herself to sleep, and Bubble's trying to drink all the wine in the world."

Billy stopped talking when the waitress brought their steaks. Billy stared at the slice of meat she placed before him, noting the apple ring and bright sprig of parsley. He slumped. "Look at that plate. I tried to kill a man, and they're trying to hand me the world on a platter. It's the sons of bitches that make it."

"I'm no SOB. And I'm going to make it." Cassie's eyes had taken on a hard glint like ice. Billy focused on his glass of champagne.

"Well, you're different, Cassie. I don't know what it is, but you're different."

After dinner they walked back to the east side under a moon that was half full and glinted off the pavement, wet from street washers. They walked in silence, Billy's mood riding him. Finally, near the river bridge, he sighed and pressed her hand.

"I'm not mad at you, baby. I know you mean well. Everyone does." Cassie returned the pressure of his hand.

"You know," he said, "you're always so sure of what you're going to do. I want to ask you something. Just a hypothetical question."

"Mr. Big Words!"

"Bull. I'm serious."

"Ask me."

"If I was maybe to enroll at the tech school here in Fayetteville. Maybe study something like plumbing or air conditioning; there's money in air conditioning." He coughed into his hand. "Could you ever see yourself staying on in this town. Maybe opening up a dance studio. Lots of little girls would love to learn to dance."

"You want to study astronomy, Billy," she quickly answered. "You don't want to install toilets the rest of your life."

"But just suppose? Like I said, a hypothetical question."

Cassie pointed into the sky. "Tell me about the moon, Billy."

TWO days later, Wilma was waiting outside the pet shop when Billy left for lunch. Still dressed in her black party dress, wrinkled now and smelling of old sweat, she was drunk; the smell of wine was all around her, and she could hardly stand. Billy tried to pass her, but she caught his arm.

"Bubble sent me," she said in a hoarse voice. "Bubble sent me to see you."

"Can't Bubble do his own talking?"

"He's sick. He asked me to come."

"Sick? What's the problem?"

"He needs to borrow some money. Just a little."

Billy lifted her hand from his sleeve. "Is he sick or drunk?"

"He's sick, Billy. Been spitting up blood. He needs some medicine."

"Medicine, my ass. More wine. Bubble knows he can go to the VA for free if he's sick."

"He just needs ten bucks."

"Where's his birdhouses? He was supposed to bring five yesterday. Tell him to bring me the birdhouses, and I'll advance him the money."

"He can't Billy. He's sick."

"No birdhouses, no money."

Wilma whimpered and slumped against the side of a car. "He's your uncle, Billy. He ain't got no money."

"And you're drunk, and I know pretty certain he is too, and it's just midday. No wonder he's broke."

"He can't build any more birdhouses. He had to pawn the saw the other day."

Billy turned, then smacked one fist into his palm. He sighed and took from his pocket a crumpled five-dollar bill. "You take this five, hear?" he said angrily. "Buy you and him some food. So help me, you better not buy any more wine. I'll be over as soon as I get off work."

Wilma stuffed the five into her bra. "He'll thank you, Billy. I know he will."

"Just remember, no wine."

She nodded, then shuffled away.

CASSIE was already fifteen minutes late leaving the bar but Billy hardly noticed, he was so deep in thought. He had gone to see Bubble immediately after work and found the two of them drinking from another jug of wine, not a scrap of food in the house. In the bathroom dried blood spotted the floor; he figured Bubble had developed ulcers. Bubble was so drunk, Billy could only get a few mumbles from him. Billy realized his uncle was out of control now, steadily getting worse, and he and Ruby would have to do something.

Finally, when Cassie was thirty minutes late, Billy began to wonder. He walked to the bar door and motioned for a waitress.

"You looking for someone," the waitress asked, cracking her gum as she looked him over.

"Yeah, Cassie. You know, the red-haired girl."

"She ain't here."

"What you mean? She leave early or something?"

"Might say that."

"Might say what?"

"You sweet on her?"

"We live together."

The waitress pursed her lips and slowly nodded. "Well, I hope I'm not fixing to break your heart, but she quit today. Said she was leaving town."

Billy felt a knot twist violently in his stomach. He swallowed loudly. "How you know she left town?"

"Said she was. She came in carrying a suitcase." The waitress took a folded paper from a pocket in her apron. "She asked me to give you this."

Billy looked into the woman's face, then at the note. He snatched it and quickly left the bar.

"Hey," the woman shouted. "Come on back tomorrow. You won't have much trouble getting another one."

Billy cleared his throat and spit in the gutter. He opened the note and began to read.

Dear Billy,

Sorry to leave so suddenly without saying good-by. It's just something I have to do. You've been very kind to me, and I appreciate it. Remember I said that our relationship had to be casual? I was becoming afraid. Little houses on the corner have a way of causing people to forget their dreams. I hope to see you again someday.

Cassie

Billy slowly crumpled the paper, then dropped it in the street. He began walking quickly toward the east side, but slowed after several blocks.

She's long gone, Billy thought. Ain't no use in hurrying. Probably been planning this for a week. Won't catch her at home or the bus station.

Billy welcomed a numbness that settled over him, a feeling almost like being drunk; he felt as if he was moving through a dense white cloud.

Billy wandered in that cloud nearly an hour through the silent streets of Haymont, past brick houses with drawn curtains, night lamps framing the windows with light. No dogs barked, they were sleeping too in their fancy kennels or close to their masters' feet. Billy walked mechanically eyes straight ahead, between the nice houses and apartments of the west side of town.

Cool air blowing from the river through cracks in the bridge made the fog begin to lift, caused his numbness to gather into an aching at the back of his throat. The ache led him to Tony's Rack Shop on Water Street.

Midnight had passed, but a crowd was still hanging around. Its buzz quieted to whispers when Billy entered.

"Gimme a shot of rye," Billy said to Tony behind the bar.

Tony filled and set a glass carefully in front of Billy. "This one's on the house, Billy," he said in a low voice. "How 'bout no trouble tonight?"

Billy drained the whiskey glass in one swallow. The rye went down rough and burning, but its heat made his throat ache less. "I didn't come here looking for any trouble, Tony. Just a few drinks."

"Atta boy." Tony slapped his arm. Billy handed him the shot glass and nodded.

With another drink in hand, Billy spun on his stool to face the crowd. "What the hell ya'll staring at?" he asked. He drank half his whiskey, peering over the rim of the glass. "Ya'll ain't

scared of Billy Riley, are you? Ain't no need to be." Many of
the people grinned stiffly. Billy finished the shot. "Anyone here
looking a fight?" There was silence. Tony fingered his beard.
Billy smiled. "Well, I ain't looking for a fight, neither. Not me.
Just some drinking with the folks I grew up with." He fished
a quarter from his pocket and flipped it to a teenaged boy
standing near the jukebox. "Hey Joey? How 'bout playing one
of them nigger songs. One that'll make us smile."

Billy spun back to the bar, the music started, and people
resumed their talk and games. The rye burned in his belly, but
it felt good and further erased the last numbness. Billy had
missed his usual late supper, so the first waves of intoxication
washed over him quickly.

"Hey, Billy, have one on me," someone said soon after. For
the next hour, Billy drank steadily and free, many people eager
to drink and talk with the baddest ass on the east side.

"You sure got Cotton Bain," one of them said. "Ran him clear
out of town."

"Johnsons been laying low, too," another said. "I ain't seen
Frankie around here in two months."

Billy just nodded and drank their offerings of beer and whiskey.

"I knew your dad well," an older man said. "Worked under
him for the past seven years. Mike was one hell of a man."

Music blared from the jukebox, snappy tunes, some of the
people danced, beers in their hands, the women heavily per-
fumed in tight jeans. Some still wore their mill uniforms, having
come here straight after second shift, their names stitched over
their left breast pocket. Smoke from their cigarettes cast the air
blue. The bar smelled of spilled beer and perfume, smoke, sweat,
pickled pig's feet and urine from the john.

After one-thirty, the crowd began to clear out. A man leaned
close to Billy so he could be heard.

"Been some guy looking for you lately," he said. "Thought
I might ought to tell you."

"Yeah? Who?"

"Big guy. He was in here earlier with two other guys. Seen him in other places, too."

"What makes you think he was looking for me?"

"No doubt he was looking for someone. Acting cocky. Not drinking much. I heard him ask Tony if he knew you."

Billy motioned for Tony to come over. "Hey, somebody been asking 'bout me tonight?"

Tony nodded. "I never saw him before. That's why I was nervous when you came in."

"What'd he look like?"

"Tall. 'Bout your size. Might have been a soldier. He had short hair."

Billy fingered the tab on his beer can. "Think I know who he is."

"Guy was wearing shades, too."

"Yep," Billy said. "Think I know just who he is."

"He trouble or something?" Tony asked.

Billy finished his beer. "Think he might be that soldier I cut down at Jerry's."

"Whooo boy. I'm glad he left before you came in."

"I wouldn't worry none about me." Billy asked for another shot of rye. "I believe I can look after myself."

"This guy looked serious," Tony said, filling a shot glass. "I'd keep my eyes open."

"You think I'm some candy ass? I've put this guy in the hospital already."

"Don't nobody think you're a candy ass," Tony answered. "You've damn sure proved that. Still, this guy wasn't fucking around. Wasn't alone, either."

Billy drained the shot glass. He was drunk and brave. "You see this clown again, just tell him to stay the fuck out of my way."

"You need any help," someone said, "let me know. Just let any of us know."

"Don't need no help." Billy was nearly the last person to leave the bar. He was roaring drunk, unsteady on his feet, and talking loud.

"How 'bout a cab?" Tony asked. "Want me to call Yellow?"

"Naw. Rather walk. I like the night air."

Billy staggered out. The numbness was over him again, but it was the numbness of alcohol. He raved in the darkness against Cassie.

"Fucking whore," he shouted toward the silent houses. "Didn't need you, anyway. Goddamn slut." He kicked a trash can clammering across the sidewalk. His shouts bounced off the walls.

"Scared you was gonna have to love someone. Weren't after yer heart, lady. Just that thing 'tween yer legs. Hear me? Sure gonna miss it."

He continued to shout, and several porch lights flipped on after he passed. Dogs barked.

"Yeah, Cassie. You didn't have to worry 'bout me taking yer heart. You never had one, bitch."

Three soldiers waited in a parked car down the alley where the streetlight was busted. They watched him come up the street, saw him stagger and heard him shout. The man wearing the shades smiled and cracked his knuckles. They waited till Billy was almost to the edge of the dark space before they got out of the car, leaving the motor idling. They waited behind trash cans against the black wall and watched him come until he was hidden from anyone's sight.

"Crazy lady," Billy shouted, but before he could finish the sentence, a pipe crashed into his kidneys. He whirled, caught the pipe again in his stomach, lost the wind from his lungs. He went down hard on his knees, his jeans ripping, the rough pavement peeling back skin. He tried to cuss, but his mouth moved silent and black.

"Feel good?" the soldier asked. "You like that?"

Billy recognized the voice and knew he was in bad, bad

trouble. His hand went to his back pocket, pulling the blade free, but the explosion of the pipe against his elbow knocked it yards across the pavement. Pain rolled up his arm and across his chest and nearly made him faint.

"You like that one, hero?" the soldier asked again. "We have more for you. All sorts of stuff."

Suddenly, Billy wasn't drunk. The pain had driven the alcohol from his brain, and his heart pounded as adrenaline poured into his blood. He looked up the street, but there was no one in sight. He tried to stand, but was knocked back by the crash of the pipe against the back of his head. Whirling, sparkling lights flew through his head until he was aware of asphalt grating against his cheek. He sucked at the air, which tasted of dust and oil. He felt a warm trickle down his neck.

"Don't kill him, man," he heard one of the soldiers say.

"Sucker don't deserve to live," the sun-shade man hissed.

Billy was pulled to his feet. Dizziness made him slump, but the soldiers kept him up and dragged him into the alley. Suddenly, he was lying against something warm, hearing a steady thump, thump, thump coming from beneath him. He realized he was being held against the hood of a car. The men still had his arms and kept him pressed down.

"Motherfuckers," Billy said, his voice weak.

"You enjoying this?" the sun-shade man asked. "I got lots of goodies planned, hero."

They tightened their grip on his arms; then Billy felt the razor as it stung, slicing through his clothes and into his back as deep as the bones. The man cut an X, shoulder blades to hips, and though Billy lunged, he was too weak to escape their grasp. The pain was hot as molten lead.

"Hey, that's enough, man!" one of them whispered.

"You got enough, brave boy?" the sun-shade man asked. "Maybe you need a little doctoring on your face?"

A police car saved Billy. It had turned into Water Street to investigate complaints of Billy's noise, with a searchlight sweeping from side to side.

"Goddamn law!" one man said, and suddenly Billy was fall-ing, hitting the pavement nose first and grinding across the surface. He heard the thump of the car's cam as it quickly pulled away, and then blackness engulfed him, and the pain went away.

13

RUBY was sleeping when the phone rang at 3 A.M. She was curled against Harold's back, but the insistent noise jolted her awake. Phones ringing late at night had always frightened her; they always brought bad news. Harold stirred, then rolled over.

"Hello," Ruby breathed into the mouthpiece.

"Is this the residence of Ruby Jean Riley?" a man's voice asked.

"Yes. Yes, it is," she answered.

"You kin to a William Thomas Riley?"

"Yes, I am." Suddenly, Ruby tasted bitterness. "He's my nephew."

"Sorry to have to bother you, ma'am, but William is in the hospital at Highsmith. I think you better come down."

"Oh, God, no," Ruby whispered. "He hurt bad? What happened?"

"You'll have to talk with the doctor about his condition. He was assaulted tonight."

Ruby left the house in her bedroom slippers.

BUBBLE was sleeping, Wilma tucked under the crook of his arm, his breaths coming in long, slow snores. Wilma rolled tighter against him, and Bubble began to dream.

He was with Mollie again at the river clearing. Six months had passed since the first time, autumn was coming, the leaves of sassafras bushes turning red. Bubble rolled over on the blanket and stared into the sky.

"I think we should leave now," he said. "I don't think I can stand to wait another week."

"But Charles, we don't have any money. Where would we go?"

"I've been thinking this thing out," he said. "Money isn't the important thing. Distance is. We'd have to go way away. As far as the West Coast. I know Mike. If he had any idea where we were, he'd come looking."

"But how would we live, honey?"

"I've thought that out, too. Lots of building is going on in California. They need draftsmen. I should get a job in a snap. I can attend school at night and finish my degree in about three years. Know what then? You can start nursing school. The heck with nursing, you can become a doctor if you want."

Mollie bent and kissed his forehead. "Charles, you make everything seem so easy."

"You want to go, don't you?"

"Yes. I mean, I want to be with you no matter where we are." Mollie bit her bottom lip. "Oh, Charles. Sometimes I feel so cheap. This is going to kill Mike."

"But you don't love him; you love me. You meant it, didn't you?"

"Yes, I meant it."

"Then, that's all that matters. We love each other. Besides, Mike will get over it. Mike's like a rock."

Mollie smiled. "You're hopeless, Charles Riley. You're a crazy, romantic, idealistic dreamer, and I do love you." She bent to kiss his lips.

Bubble's dream faded, then jumped ahead in time two weeks. He was with Mollie again, driving a dirt road through the countryside. Molly was unusually quiet, staring through the car window at passing fields.

"So what is it, baby?" he asked. "It can't be that terrible. Does Mike know about us?"

"No."

"Then what's the matter? You haven't changed your mind about leaving, have you?"

"No."

"Hey, look at me. I know you didn't call me away from work just to joyride."

Mollie cleared her throat. "I'm pregnant, Charles."

"What!" Bubble felt his stomach twist.

"I've been late, and I saw a doctor yesterday. He said I'm pregnant."

"Oh God. I thought you were sure you were safe?"

"I thought so, too."

Bubble found he was driving only twenty miles an hour and pulled to the side to let a car pass. He felt sick. Mollie was smoothing her skirt over her belly.

"Well, it doesn't matter. It's not his baby. I know it."

Mollie didn't answer.

"We'll still leave." He stroked her cheek. "Nothing has to change, baby."

Mollie slowly shook her head. "I'm pregnant, Charles. We have no money. We're going to have to wait."

Bubble's dream changed again and now he was standing on a high cliff, alone, overlooking the Pacific Ocean. In his hands he held a tiny baby, so small he cradled the child in his palms. The baby was pink and sleeping. Suddenly, a wind rose from the cliff and swept the infant from his hands, carrying it high into the sky until it was only a spot that nearly vanished. Then it began to fall. The spot became larger until he could make out features, Billy, full grown, flailing his arms as he fell, shouting.

"Bubble, help me," Billy shouted. "Help me!"

Billy was falling to the rocks beneath the cliff and Bubble rushed to catch him, but the wind rose again and pushed him back like a strong current. Billy loomed larger, tumbling, his cries for help shrill and long.

Bubble woke up hard, struggling against the heavy quilt. He threw the covers to his feet and sat up in bed. His heart pounded.

He heard a car horn blowing from in front of the house, then footsteps coming quickly up the porch steps. A rap on the door followed. Bubble swung off the bed and weaved through the darkness to the door. Wallace stood there.

"Thought I never would wake you up," Wallace said.

"What the hell's the matter?"

"It's Billy. He's been beat up real bad. Ruby sent me to get you."

WHEN the blackness settled over Billy, he welcomed it, a gentle, formless end to his pain. He felt he was rising with incredible speed, as if the heavens had opened and he was flying into some great expanse without light or noise or physical sensation.

So, this is what it's like to die, he thought, but he wasn't afraid, wasn't even particularly curious, just glad that he no longer hurt so bad. In the darkness, only his mind existed, and time became something without meaning or passage. He could have been floating in the blackness for hundreds of years, maybe minutes or just fractions of seconds. It didn't matter.

The light began as a pinpoint, as singularly and focused as one star against a very black sky. It swam in the blackness, seemed to move against the background, or maybe there was only a feeling of movement, for he had nothing to measure against, but the light shimmered and grew. The star increased in brilliance until it shone like Venus hanging in the western sky. Just like Venus, Billy thought, the same blue splinters around the edges and the cold, silver center. I wonder if Venus is really God?

Then the point of light changed again, the splinters drawing in, the blue fading to white, the light drawing into a tiny, silver crescent. It is Venus, Billy thought.

Suddenly, he was aware of something round and cool pressing against where his eye had been, and he felt the blush of a breeze where he remembered his cheek and he smelled the fragrance of wisteria blossoms. He lifted his eye from the lens piece of a telescope to discover Bubble standing beside him.

"Venus goes through phases, see, just like the moon," Bubble said, peering at the planet through the branches of a budding sweetgum tree.

"Boy, this is neat," young Billy said. "I never would have thought it would look like this."

Bubble smiled, then pointed at another object in the sky. "There's lots of things to see in the heavens, son. We'll learn all sorts of things."

Billy felt his uncle's hand on his shoulder. "I bet Dad would like to see. I bet he would love to see this." Billy pointed at the house, but the driveway was still empty.

Then there was only blackness again, Bubble was gone, the telescope, nothingness and the point of light.

It's true, Billy thought, your life does pass before you when you die. The good times.

The light again grew brighter until the brilliance became an orb, the orb slowly transforming into a person, miniature, but rushing towards him. At last, he could see it was a girl; she was twirling and leaping; finally he recognized Cassie.

In her red and silver leotards, she danced in circles around him, beckoning with her hands for him to follow. Her lips were moving, but her words were silent, her mouth moving frantically like a fish pulled from water. She seemed so eager for him to come, was smiling and pointing at the place where the light shone. She circled once more, then began to recede. He read her lips.

"Come with me, Billy. Just follow me. Life's so easy if you'll just be like me."

Billy wanted to follow her into the light, but as he struggled, hands surrounded him. The hands pushed him back gently but firmly. They weren't bad hands, just the hands of working people, calloused and weathered and strong. He could still see Cassie urging him to come until she slowly shrank back into the orb of light.

When the light grew again, this time it became a face—bright blue eyes and thick, red hair: his father. Mike's face was bright as the sun against the blackness.

"Get up from there, son. Stand right up." Mike's voice was even and controlled as always.

Billy tried to answer, but where he remembered his mouth had been there was only a dark space and no sound.

"You can get up from there. Any Riley ever worth his salt could stand up no matter how hard they knocked you down."

Mike's face shimmered and faded, then changed into the figure of Ruby. She stood before him in her white linen waitress's uniform, gazing upon him with pity. She raised her hands over him and twigs began to grow from her finger tips, dividing into branches, thickening into massive limbs. The canopy of an oak tree spread above her, leaves budded and clusters of acorns formed. Her legs and torso swelled into a tree trunk, weathered and mighty, only her face remaining unchanged. She continued to smile at him with great love and sympathy.

When the light changed again, he was back in the yard with Bubble.

"Can you see it, son?" He was pointing into the southern sky. "Right over there. The yellow one."

Billy followed Bubble's arm but only saw dark sky. "I can't see it," he tried to say. "I can't see it, Bubble."

"You have to look hard, son. She's not very bright, but she's beautiful. Saturn is the prettiest one."

The light changed once more and receded into a pinpoint. Suddenly, Billy was afraid because for the first time he felt pain, intense pain that washed through where he remembered his limbs.

"I can't see it yet, Bubble," he shouted, and this time he heard his voice, though very low and distant. "I don't see it yet." The point of light came closer; the pain was worse. Ruby's face reappeared, and though it shimmered like before, this time she was surrounded by a halo of light.

THE doctor drew back, taking the penlight from in front of Billy's eye. "He's coming out of it," he said to Ruby.

Ruby held Billy's hand while he mumbled and rolled his head from side to side. His lids fluttered, then opened.

"I can't see it yet," he mumbled.

"Can't see what, honey?" Ruby squeezed his hand harder. "Billy, this is Ruby. It's me, Ruby."

Billy blinked against the harsh light. Ruby, a doctor? he thought. Where am I?

"Don't try to talk yet," Ruby said. "Wait till you feel better."

"You're going to be all right, son," the doctor said. "You just need rest. I'm going to give you something that will help you sleep a little longer."

Billy felt someone touch his other hand. "Bubble," he whispered. "Where's the telescope?"

"You just sleep, Billy. Everything's going to be fine."

"Guess I ain't in heaven," Billy said to Ruby, " 'cause Bubble is here."

Ruby watched his eyes flutter again, then close, and her own eyes clouded with tears. She knew then he would be all right.

14

BILLY was young and strong, and in two days he was off the critical list and resting comfortably in a private room paid for by the VA. Ruby had sat with him every minute she wasn't working, fussing over him, feeding him and seeing that he was looked after. Bubble even stayed sober those two days and looked the best he had in months.

Billy's right arm was fractured and he wore a sling. He had a deep cut on his head, a slight concussion, and three broken ribs. His back was hurt worst, the X cut long and deep, but the wounds were healing and would only take a matter of time. Billy was lucky; he knew it, the doctors knew it, everyone said so. The police car had swept its light over him in passing and had backed up. He was bleeding so badly, there was no attempt to chase the fleeing car. The doctors had kept the police away until now.

Early in the afternoon, Wallace came into the room, followed by a detective.

"You're sure looking better." Wallace shook Billy's good hand. "Couple of days ago, you had me worried."

"Couple of days ago, I was worried."

"Aw, you'll be out of here in a week's time," Wallace said and ruffled Billy's hair. The detective was standing back out of the way. Wallace introduced him. "Billy, this is Detective Jerry Brown. He's an old friend of mine."

The detective stepped forward and shook Billy's hand. Billy nodded, but only in politeness. He'd been dreading this moment.

"Howdy, Billy. Glad to hear you're getting better."

Again, Billy nodded.

"Billy," Wallace began in his best court room voice. "Detective Brown wants to ask you about the person or persons who assaulted you. I'll see to it personally that they are arrested."

Billy closed his eyes and leaned against the pillow. He heard the rustle of paper as the detective opened his notebook.

"Who did this to you, Billy?" he asked. "I'm just here to help you."

Billy stared at one of the potted plants. "I don't know who did it. It was dark."

"Aw, come on, Billy," Wallace said. "You don't expect me to believe that, do you?"

The detective waved at Wallace to be quiet. "Son, you must have seen something. They had to be mighty close. Now think a minute." He lowered his voice. "Who did it?"

Billy turned up his palm. "Honest. It could have been anyone. I know there were three, maybe four, but I didn't see any faces."

For the next half hour Wallace and the detective tried to persuade Billy to name someone. He stuck to his story. Finally, the detective snapped closed his notebook.

"Well, if you can't identify anyone, then there's no way I can help you." Wallace went with the detective into the hall. When he came back, his face was red with anger. "O.K., big shot," he said, sitting on the bed. "Why you have to play this game?"

"What game?" Billy said with wide eyes.

"I know damn well it was that soldier who got you. Hell fire, everyone on the east side knows it."

"It wasn't just him. There was two others. He'd never done it alone."

"So, why're you protecting him? Umph? Why the hell don't you let us arrest him? He nearly killed you."

"And I nearly killed him the first time. I'm calling it even."

Wallace bit off a hangnail and spit it on the floor. He cocked his head. "Is it going to stay even? Are you going to let it die? There's already talk in the bars of what you'll do to him as soon as you're well."

"Don't nobody make my plans for me."

"I wish I could believe you. God, I do. I wish I could believe that you're going to leave this town and go to school or whatever the hell it is you want to do."

"I can take care of myself."

"Then do it, umph. 'Cause I can't help you any longer." Wallace left without looking back.

Ruby came later that night, still wearing her uniform. She brought him two pork chop sandwiches and a milk shake from the diner.

"You're looking better every time I come in here," she said, as she tucked the covers around his feet. "Couple more days, and I bet you'll be clawing at the door to get out of here."

"I'd leave right now, if they'd let me. They're starving me to death." He unwrapped one of the sandwiches and took a bite.

"Well, it won't be long now. The doctor says you can probably leave at the end of the week."

"I gotta get back to work."

"You don't worry about work. I talked with Mr. Banner, and he said that if it took a month for you to get well, you'd still have a job."

"I'd rather work than lie in bed. I can't even sleep at night."

Ruby gently fluffed the pillows. "Bet your back is sore as four boils." Then she put fresh water in the flower vases and stacked Billy's magazines.

"Why don't you go ahead and ask me 'bout her," he said between mouthfuls, "before you clean this place to death."

"Ask what, honey?"

"Come on, Ruby. I know you like I know my foot. Ask me why Cassie left."

Ruby took a long time rearranging flowers. "I didn't think it was none of my business."

Billy unwrapped the second sandwich. "She just left, that's all. I guess she went on up to New York to try and make it as a dancer. There wasn't any love between us, anyway."

"She didn't have anything to do with you getting hurt, did she?" Ruby's eyes blazed. "So help me, if she did, I'll find that little hussy and, and —!"

"Calm down," Billy interrupted. "She had nothing to do with that."

"Well, it's better she's gone, anyway, Billy. A woman couldn't be made of much that would dance like she did in one of them places. You just forget her, 'cause you're a heap better off."

Billy tried to suck his milk shake through the straw, but it was too thick. He took off the lid and scooped the ice cream with his fingers. It was cold on his tongue, and though he tried to think coldly of Cassie, he remembered most how her eyes would shine as she talked of one day dancing on Broadway.

"She was O.K. Ruby," Billy said. "I don't have any hard feelings against her."

"Well, you put her up for two months. She owed you, and then skip out without even saying thank you or good-bye."

"You know, Ruby, I was getting a few benefits from her being around. It wasn't just her taking."

"Well, that doesn't matter none," Ruby said and flushed. "But, I tell you, honey, you're a lot better off without her."

"Ruby, you remember how you're all the time telling me you want me to find something I have an interest in and go for it?"

"Yeah. Not in them exact words."

"Well, just look at Cassie this way. She was one lady who came for a while, knew exactly what she wanted, and went."

BILLY left the hospital at the end of the week and went to recuperate at Ruby's house. He was still terribly sore and often had headaches, but he was happy to be out of the hospital. He spent the first day shuffling around the house and yard, trying to limber his limbs. Thanksgiving was the next week, and Ruby was busy getting things ready, the fragrance of spices and fruit mingling with the pungent odors of late fall. The summer birds had flown south, leaving only starlings and wrens and blackbirds. The east side was even drabber than usual, the few flowers withered, tree branches as barren and stark as animal bones.

Billy's mood was also gray. He was ashamed that he had allowed himself to begin to love someone who had been honest and straightforward in her intentions all along. The beating—he couldn't face that, yet, so he shelved it in the back of his mind and tried to lose the memory in grayness.

Ruby pampered him and fed him and tried to bring back his smile.

"Have another piece," she said, scooping up another slice of pie. "Lord, you're still skinny as a rail."

"Good God. Stop! I'm going to bust if you keep on."

"You need to eat. Ain't nothing healthier for a person than good, hot apple pie."

Billy stuck the slice of pie with his fork. "Speaking of healthy, what did the doctor say when Bubble saw him the other day? You didn't answer last time I asked."

Ruby stirred more sugar into her coffee, the spoon tinkling against the sides of the cup. Her forehead wrinkled. "He ain't good. Not good at all."

"What did the doctor say?"

"Oh, lots of stuff. Said he has an ulcer. Said his liver is swollen. Told him he better stop drinking—right now."

"It doesn't surprise me," Billy answered. "I've been telling him the same thing."

"Everyone's been telling him, but he's gonna drink right on, no matter what."

Billy laid his fork aside. "You know, maybe he's starting to wise up. The last couple of times he came by, I couldn't smell wine on him."

Ruby slowly shook her head. "He's drinking, honey. He

can't fool me. I think he's started drinking vodka to hide the odor."

Billy pushed the saucer of pie away and leaned back into his chair. "I gotta do something. He has this crazy idea that he's going to make me stop drinking by killing himself."

"That's pure nonsense. You don't let his idiotic talk make you feel you're to blame. I've been expecting this to happen to him for years."

"Well, I can't understand it. Bubble's never done nothing but good things for people and look at him."

"I shouldn't have told you. Don't worry yourself over Bubble. He ain't worth it. Just concentrate on getting well." Ruby slid the saucer back in front of Billy.

"Will you lighten up? You're feeding me to death."

"Just eat this last piece."

THANKSGIVING dawn a sharp wind from out of the north ripped the last leaves from branches. The mill was closed, so there wasn't the usual back odor of burning coal, only the fragrance of hot pies and stuffed turkeys baking. Ruby rose with the sun to finish her cooking. When Billy got up and came into the kitchen, there was a pitcher of hot mulled wine on the stove.

"I know it's early," Ruby said, "but if we have any, we'll have to drink it now. I don't intend to have any in the house when Bubble gets here."

From Billy's earliest memory, Ruby had hosted Thanksgiving dinner for the family. She always invited several people from the community who she thought worthy or needing. This year it was Mr. Banner, a widower for five years, and Harold, of course, Wilma, and old Mr. Royster from the rest home. The crowd began to arrive at noon, bundled in coats and mufflers, and warmed themselves in front of the oil heater, sipping hot cranberry juice and watching a football game on television. Everyone patted Billy's arm and asked how he was feeling, but there was no mention of the fight. Bubble and Wilma arrived last. Their cheeks were rosy, but Billy and Ruby knew it wasn't from the cold. Wilma went to help Ruby in the kitchen while the men discussed sports, though loudly, so Mr. Royster could hear.

At Ruby's invitation, everyone crowded around the table. Ruby said grace, then told everyone to sit down. There was the usual coughing and tinkling of silverware as each waited for another to begin.

"Well, dig in ya'll," Bubble said. "Whoever eats the fastest, gets the most." They began passing plates to Billy, who was serving. Suddenly, Billy grabbed the carving knife and plunged it into the turkey's breast.

"Forgot all about this," he exclaimed, and began slicing, but not before feeling a twinge in his chest. Mike had always carved the turkey.

The food was good and there was plenty of it: turkey with cornbread stuffing and cranberries and mashed potatoes and giblet gravy and butter beans cooked with salt pork and fresh collards and glasses of cold, sweet tea. They followed with pumpkin pie and pineapple cake and coffee. By then they were all patting their stomachs and trying not to belch and swearing they had just eaten the best meal in a year.

Harold was especially complimentary. "I swear it. I ain't ate like this in ten years I know."

Ruby's face beamed. "Well, we're just glad you could be here. Imagine having to eat Thanksgiving dinner in some old truck-stop diner."

"Meal like this, Billy," Mr. Banner said, "ought to make your arm good as new."

"It nearly is. I'm planning on coming back to work next week."

"You just take your time. It'll be a couple more weeks before the Christmas season picks up."

People began leaving around three. Wallace stopped by to

say hello and have a slice of pie. Bubble and Wilma waited until the football game was over before leaving.

"He looked O.K.," Billy said to Ruby when he was gone. "Hadn't had more than a shot or two before he got here."

"Well, if wishes come true, he'll never taste another drop."

Billy cut himself another piece of pie. "I feel good about things, Ruby, you know? I think the ole boy is going to come to his senses."

After Billy finished shaving that afternoon he noticed his bottle of Aqua Velva was missing from the medicine chest. "Hey Ruby," he shouted. "You seen my after-shave?"

"Ain't got none," Harold answered, "I can loan you mine."

"I'll look," Ruby shouted. Billy heard her rummaging around in his bedroom, then through the kitchen cabinet. When she came into the bathroom, her face was pale.

"Bubble must a' took it," she said, her words slow as a sigh. "The rubbing alcohol is missing. So is my vanilla flavoring."

Ruby was twisting her dishcloth in her hands. Billy's stomach went sour.

BILLY returned to work the following Monday. He found the rats and fish and puppies even more boring than before, now that he no longer had Cassie. Two more acceptance letters to colleges arrived that week. He put them away for the time being and didn't tell Ruby. After the doctor took the stitches from his back, he returned to his apartment for the first time since his beating.

Billy opened the front door with dread, expecting to find Cassie's ghost in every room. She had left nothing, no clothes, or posters, no long red hairs in the bathroom, not even her smell upon the sheets. She was gone, as if she had never existed, the apartment musty smelling and cold.

Billy had continued to push all thoughts of his beating into the back of his mind until Tony the barman stopped by. Billy opened his front door to find him standing there holding a paper sack.

"Hey Tony. What you know?"

"Just wanted to stop by and see how you were," Tony answered. "Sorry I didn't get by the hospital, but I been pretty busy."

"No problem. You couldn't hardly find a chair for all the flowers."

Tony took a seat, then pulled a six-pack from the sack. "Wanna beer? I brought this for you."

"Sure. Open one for each of us."

"I didn't know if you were taking medicine or something and couldn't drink."

They sat at the table and downed a couple of beers each, discussing things going on around the east side. Tony seemed nervous, and stared at the table a lot.

" 'Bout that fight you were in," Tony finally said. "You mind talking about it?"

"What's there to talk about? I got the hell beat out of me," Billy shrugged.

"I felt real bad, Billy. Like it was maybe my fault for giving you so much whiskey that night."

"Forget that. I'd have bought it from someone else if not from you." Billy tapped the top of his can. "I guess there's a lot of talk, umph?"

"Aw, just stories. You know how people like to talk up a fight."

"I don't figure it's anyone else's business."

"Oh, you're right about that. Damn straight. Still, you know how people talk."

Billy knew he could no longer dodge reality. He reached into the refrigerator for another beer. "Yeah, well tell me some of the talk. I guess the Johnsons and Bains are laughing their asses off?"

"Not really. Maybe it would have been different if this

guy was local, but he ain't. Just some ass-hole soldier."

"What's he saying? Anyone seen him?"

"Yeah. About everyone has. He's been hanging around some of the bars talking a lot of shit."

"Let him talk. He knows it took three of them to get me."

"Everyone knows that, Billy. Your reputation ain't suffered none. Ain't a person on the east side that doesn't think you could take him again one on one."

"Again?" Billy asked, raising one eyebrow. He dreaded what was coming next as much as he had ever dreaded anything. "So, the next card is mine. Is that what you're getting at, Tony? Everybody's waiting to see when I'm going for revenge?"

"Hell, I don't know, Billy. You know how people like a fight."

"I'm well aware of that. Especially when they're not on the receiving end."

"Billy, it's just that you have a reputation around here. Ex-Marine, your old man a war hero and all. People don't like to see no outsider get the best of one of the home boys."

Billy turned up his can and drank loudly. "You know I'm on probation. Another arrest and I'll probably pull time."

"Nobody wants that, Billy. By the way, that was pretty damn honorable of you not to press charges."

"I figured we were even. That's all."

"Most people say you just wanted him out of jail so you could get at him."

"People. To hell with most people. Anybody ask—tell them Billy Riley is calling it even."

Tony held up his hands. "Hey, fine with me. I don't want to see you fighting no more. Problem is, this guy is pushing it again. He knows he didn't win that rematch fairly."

"Even. I won the first. He can take the second. I won't count his buddies."

Tony chewed his thumbnail. His disappointment was clear to Billy.

"Goddamn it, Tony. What can I do? You wanna hear something crazy? I've nearly made up my mind to go to college. I fight this guy and everything's down the drain."

"I'm with you, Billy. We've been friends a long time." Tony lowered his voice. "I just know what people are going to say. That's all."

"Well, it's even. Anyone ask you, I say it's an even ball game."

THE next day, Bubble was on his way back from Willie's with a jug when the jacked-up Chevy passed, stopped and backed up. Bubble was staggering drunk but recognized the soldier and cussed him.

The soldier smiled while stepping from his car. He slapped Bubble hard across his mouth, knocking him to the pavement and shattering the wine bottle. Bubble tried to stand, but the soldier put him back down with a shoe to the ribs. A trickle of blood started from the corner of Bubble's mouth. A crowd was gathering on the sidewalk.

"Tell that chicken-shit hero of yours that I'm waiting on him," the soldier said. "Ask him where his guts went."

Tony and three more locals were standing on Billy's apartment steps that evening waiting for him to come home. Billy knew by the way they walked to meet him that something was up.

"That soldier slapped Bubble around this afternoon," Tony said. The others nodded. "Kicked him, too."

Billy felt dizzy, a tingling spreading across his face. "Did he hurt him?" Billy hissed through clinched jaws. "So help me God, if he did, I'll kill that son of a bitch!"

"He didn't hurt him much. Just busted his lip. But, he's after you, Billy. Like I told you, he don't want it even."

Billy was so mad his legs trembled and felt weak. He felt an odd sensation of falling, and a vivid image of the rat entangled in the parachute cords flashed through his mind. When he spoke, his voice was hollow and without emotion, as if coming from the bottom of a deep, deep pit. "Doctor said two weeks from this Saturday my arm would be good for whatever. Go tell that bastard he can name the place. Nighttime, no cops and no charges afterwards. We'll settle this little matter once and for all."

Tony slapped Billy's shoulder. One of the men turned up his thumb. The news spread like wildfire through the east side, from bar to bar, to the snack room at the mill and back to the streets. Billy Riley was out for blood.

15

BUBBLE passed out for the night soon after he arrived home. The next morning his lip was swollen and sore and he had to ask Wilma what had happened.

"It was that soldier guy who beat up Billy. He hit you a couple of times."

Bubble wished he hadn't asked then because he knew the implications. "Oh, God," he moaned. He found his wine bottle empty on the kitchen table.

"We have anything to drink around here? I need something."

"There ain't nothing, Bubble. You drank all the wine when you got home."

He began looking through the cabinet, then in the trash can for empty bottles. "God knows I gotta have a drink of something."

"Bubble, honey. You gotta stop drinking that shaving lotion and stuff. It's gonna hurt you."

"Mind your own business, woman. Since when can you talk to someone about drinking too much?" He took a bottle from the trash and drained the few drops in the bottom. Then, from one pocket he fished out a dollar bill and some change. "Goddamn money. I don't know where it goes to."

Wilma stared at the money and nervously licked her lips. "Bubble, we gotta get some money from somewhere. Your landlord came by yesterday and said we have to pay the rent by Friday or get out."

"Fuck the landlord."

"We're gonna need this place, Bubble. Winter's coming on. We need it more than we need more wine."

Bubble slammed the bottle back into the barrel. It shattered against another bottle.

"Then get your ass out and go to work. Start whoring or something. I don't care what you do; just get off my back." He stuffed the money back into his pocket and headed for the door.

"But we're gonna lose the house," Wilma wailed after him. Bubble slammed the door. Wilma laid her head on the table and began to cry softly.

BUBBLE bought his pint from Willie, then decided to join the few bums that were hanging around in back. They sat against the back wall enjoying the weak sunlight.

"Ain't seen you in a while," Chubby said, his face wrinkling with a smile. "Why you been hiding out?"

"Ain't been hiding." Bubble slid down the wall between two of the men. "Had things to do." He unscrewed the bottle lid and drank while the winos stared.

"You still trying to drink all the wine in the world?"

The wine burned Bubble's ulcer, but the burning was better than the torment in his head. The alcohol hit his bloodstream quickly and he was already beginning to feel better.

"I've expanded the project. I'm drinking anything these days."

"You got any to spare?"

Reluctantly, Bubble passed the bottle. When it came back, he sucked at it again.

"I hear Wilma's been living with you?" Chubby asked. "Makes nights better, don't she?"

Bubble grunted. "Damn woman's running me broke. She can drink more wine than I can."

The winos chuckled. "She always could. Why 'da hell you think Punk left her?"

Shorty, the oldest of the winos, studied Bubble's face. "You ain't looking so good, Bubble," finally he said. "Ya don't look good at all."

"I got an ulcer that's been acting up." He tried to hide the twitch that had begun recently on his left side.

"Got a twitch, too, I see. You need to slow down some, son. You're going too fast. Way too fast."

"I've never known you to turn down a drink," Bubble answered.

"Nope. Never have and never will. I'll sure own up to that. But the difference in me is this, son. If there's a drink handy, I take it. If there ain't, I don't go looking for one."

"You're still a bum, Shorty."

Shorty held up one finger and nodded his head. "Yep, a bum but not an alkie. Bums take what comes to them, and they don't own nothing and nothing owns them. Alkies, it's different. Whiskey owns them and kills them."

"Ain't much difference. We all gonna die, anyway."

"True, but I'm sixty-four and can still get it up. Alkies die lying in their own puke."

Bubble shrugged and lifted his bottle. As drunkenness settled over him, the pain in his belly eased and his twitch lessened. Again, he passed the bottle.

"You're a good man," Shorty said. "Always been just as kind and generous. I'd hate to see your health get down. Man ain't got nothing more valuable than his health."

The pint was quickly drained, and the four men pooled their coins for a half gallon. They spent the rest of the morning passing the jug and talking. About noon, Teddy Banks, who'd hung out with Billy in high school, was taking the shortcut behind the store and stopped when he saw Bubble.

"Hey Bubble. What you doing hanging out with these bums?"

"Eat shit, kid," said Chubby.

"I'm just minding my business," Bubble answered. "More than I can say for you."

"Don't get riled up. I just wanted to ask how Billy's doing."

"Billy? Crazy. Crazy as a damn loon."

"Well, tell him I'm pulling for him, hear? I hope he takes that soldier's head off."

"What the hell you talking 'bout?" He stuffed the jug between his knees.

"What do you mean, what am I talking about? You gotta know Billy and that soldier are tangling again Saturday week."

Bubble spit in the dirt. "So, what else ain't new. I've washed my hands of that boy. I don't care if he fights King Kong."

Bubble left the wall soon after and went straight home and sold the rear tires off his jacked-up car. He and Wilma reached the proper state of numbness by nightfall.

Bubble hallucinated regularly now when drunk. Sometimes he imagined there was a dog crossing the street in front of him; sometimes a bat would circle the kitchen light while he sat drinking, but usually he saw Mike's face. The face would appear over the cabinet or outside a window, flickering at first, then strengthening to a pale green glow. At first, the hallucinations hadn't bothered him; he knew they were a product of the wine and would pass. But in past weeks he had begun to worry that he had crossed a threshold into a realm where there was no reality, that maybe Mike could return from the grave to haunt him.

"What the hell you want now?" Bubble said when the face appeared again, hovering over the sink. He reached and shook Wilma, trying to rouse her from her stupor. "See there," he said. "Can't tell me that I been seeing things." Wilma groaned but didn't wake. Bubble stared back into Mike's face, which changed briefly into that of a grinning dog, then back again.

"I told you not to be coming 'round here no more," Bubble said. "Dead men are supposed to stay in their grave."

Mike looked on with his usual patience.

"You're dead and I don't have to listen to you no more." Bubble stuck a finger in each ear. Still, when Mike talked, Bubble heard his words as if a loudspeaker was attached to each ear.

"Drunk again, I see. You ever been anything other than a drunk?"

"I've been lots of things, but I've never been no son of a bitch like you."

Mike frowned. "Thinking back, I can't remember many days when you stayed sober."

"I don't remember many days when you weren't a son of a bitch."

"I give you a month at the most," Mike said. "You ought to see that liver of yours. It can go at any time. You have that twitch, too, just like old drunks get right before they croak."

In defiance, Bubble lifted his bottle and guzzled. "Ain't nothing to dying. One thing's for sure, we won't be in the same place."

"That's true. They keep the winners and losers separated, you know."

"What'd you ever win 'cept that medal of yours? You ain't even got that in your pocket now. Ain't even got no pockets."

"Now I have peace. That's enough. Peace, because before I went I had respect, a good job, house and money in the bank."

"You forgetting the boy? Or does he come under the category of respect? That's all you ever allowed him to have of you, respect. Hell, them bird dogs of yours respected you."

"I loved Billy. His respect just came naturally."

"Love on a ten-foot pole."

"I gave Billy what he needed to survive out there. I gave him grit and determination and a damn good left jab. Hugging is nice, but when the shit starts flying that good, sharp jab is going to help you more than hugs."

"You think that jab is gonna help him next week? They're gonna be slinging hawkbills, not jabs."

"I took everything they ever threw at me. Billy will come out all right."

"Damn right he's gonna come out all right, 'cause I'm gonna save him."

Mike laughed. "You're going to save him?"

"Damn right. Think I'm drinking all this shit for nothing? He'll see the light."

"That's a good front, Bubble, but you can't die for him. I already have."

"Stop trying to take credit where it ain't due. You died for your reputation, for that goddamn mill. I'm dying for Billy."

Mike laughed so hard, his image flickered, then changed into a cat, then a pig before changing back to Mike. "He's my son, Bubble. You might have hugged him more, but he was born from me."

Bubble took the wine bottle and flung it toward Mike. The glass shattered against the wall, red wine splattering on the boards and flowing down. Mike flickered again, changing into the image of a huge bat with long talons. The streams of wine were now dripping blood. Bubble shut his eyes till the horror was gone.

"There's things you don't know," Bubble shouted at the spot where Mike had been. "There's a lot you don't know, and if I was the man I'd tell you." He laid his face on the table. "There's things you don't know," he shouted and began to sob. "And if I was the man. If I was just the man."

16

THE east side rocked with news of the coming fight. In two days most every storekeeper, millworker, street bum and kid had heard at least three different versions of what was to take place. Not long after, the police knew, as well as Wallace and Ruby.

Wallace was parked outside of Billy's apartment when he came home from work. Billy hesitated at the corner when he saw the car, but then went ahead, knowing he would have to face Wallace sooner or later. Wallace just nodded when Billy shook his hand and said nothing till they were inside. "What's this shit I hear about you?"

"I don't know what you've heard. Hey, you want a beer?" He spent several seconds rummaging in the refrigerator."

"No, I don't want a beer. Hell yeah, give me one. You really going to fight this guy, Billy?" Wallace's face was gray as marble.

Billy settled into a chair and took a long breath. He looked Wallace in the eye. "I don't know what I'm going to do, man. Honest I don't."

"Well, everyone else in town seems to know what you're going to do. It's the hottest talk I've heard in years."

Billy took one sip of beer, then set the can far away. "It doesn't seem that I have much choice, Wallace. Seems like fate has it all arranged for me."

"Fate, hell. Nothing but bull-headed pride is making you fight."

"Yeah, well what would you do if you were me? You know,

the Rileys have a reputation in these parts. I can't just walk away from the guy. Especially after what he did to Bubble."

"I'll tell you what you can do. You can pack your bags and get out of this town and start doing something with your life. That's what you can do. What that soldier thinks wouldn't slow me down for one second."

Billy leaned forward and began to pick specks of lint from his jeans. "It ain't—it ain't that easy, Wallace. I can't just run away from this fight. I'd be letting a lot of people down."

Wallace's face reddened and he gripped his chair arm. "Letting people down? My God, Billy! All you'll let down is a bunch of street bums and cutthroats. What about Ruby and Bubble, hell, even me? You think by not fighting you'll be letting us down? You think we want you to kill that man?"

"Who said anything about killing? All we're going to do is settle this matter."

Wallace rose suddenly and walked over to a table in the corner. On the table was a small egg-shaped glass ball filled with water. Inside was a tiny, plastic snowman and bits of synthetic snow that swirled when the ball was shaken. Wallace stared into the glass for several seconds. "Getting ready for Christmas, umph. Billy, I'm trying to be rational. If I remember correctly, the first time you two tangled, he went to the hospital. The second time, you went. Third time, I'd bet it doesn't stop short of the morgue. I figure you'll either end up dead or charged with premeditated murder. I don't know which is worse."

Billy piled the bits of lint in a mound on his knee. "A lot you're saying may be true, Wallace. Right now, I don't know. I do know this—some things are going to happen whether you like it or not."

Wallace returned to the table. "I never knew you to take much stock in predestination. Sounds like an easy out to me."

Billy shrugged.

"I could revoke your parole, Billy. Wouldn't take nothing but signing a piece of paper. Let this ride out while you're in jail."

Wallace slowly shook his head. "I'm not, though. You've got to face up to your life sooner or later. I had to; so does everyone. It's cut and dry with me. You fight or you don't. Dead in the ground or dead in prison, I couldn't help you either way." Wallace drained his beer. "You have the world at your feet, son. Wouldn't be much of a choice to me."

Wallace left Billy at the table adding to his pile of lint.

Street talk on the east side told the story different. Billy Riley was fully redeemed from his beating in the eyes of most people. It was one thing to take a beating, but it was another to come back for revenge. To the teenage street idlers, his stature grew daily.

"Hey, Billy, you're gonna kick that mother's ass."

"Got my money on you, homeboy. Bet that sucker don't last one minute. You gonna put war on his ass."

Billy drank free beer in the bars and listened to endless advice about how to fight the soldier and where they could meet out of eyesight of the cops. The days passed quickly and Billy grew stronger and fast like before. Still, as his health returned, amid the back slaps and pledges of support, his legs often felt numb as if he were standing in the cold waters of a rapidly flowing stream.

BILLY went to the third therapy session because he had to. He entered the room angrily and sat rigid in the tall-backed chair. The clock ticked loudly in his ear.

"What do I want to do with my life, umph? What kind of a dumb question is that?"

"Just a straight question, Billy. Where would you like to see yourself ten years from now?"

Billy thought of the sprawling, gray, crumbling community that sat like a checkerboard outside the walls of the mill. He saw the people who lived there, faces as gray as the houses they rented, whose lives were measured in units of Friday afternoon till Monday morning. He felt strongly the ropes that bound him to the east side, bonds that seemed to be pulling stronger every day.

"Ten years is a long time. I don't see much use in anyone looking that far ahead. I might be dead in ten years."

"But you'll probably be alive. You're a young healthy man. What would you like to imagine yourself doing?"

Billy remembered the game he had played with Cassie where she had him imagine people he would like to be. "It's not what I want to be," he said. "That's not the way it works."

"How does it work?"

"It's not what you want to be; it's what they want you to be. That's the way things turn out."

"Not necessarily, Billy. I've seen your records. You've got a good head on your shoulders. Could do most anything you'd like. Why do you think you're controlled by other people?"

Billy rose and walked to the window. He pulled up the blinds, letting light flood the room. He blinked at the sudden brightness, then returned to the chair. "That's a lot better. I've never understood why you guys like the dark so well."

The doctor waited, drumming two fingers against his temple.

"I guess we have a choice in the beginning. Right at the very start. Ya know, whether we want to be the Jesse James type or Billy Graham. Brains matter some too—hard to be a dentist if you're cut out to haul garbage. Still, the problem starts for everyone soon as they make that first move."

The doctor settled back into his chair and lit a cigarette. He offered Billy one. "What do you mean by making the first move?"

"Well, it's sort of like a checkers game. That's what it's like. Your first move is free as a bird, preacher or outlaw, all the options are there. But, after you take that first move, then the game begins, and from then on it's a ball game. You follow me?"

"I think so. Go on."

"Every move from then on is an attempt to stay on top. No freedom after that. You're trying to outsmart some guy who's trying to outsmart you."

"So, you're afraid to take your first move? Is that what you mean? Afraid that the game you get involved in will turn out to be something you don't like?"

Billy stared at the tree outside the window. The bare branches were being whipped by the late fall wind. "I'm not afraid of nothing. It's just that I see through it all. Maybe a sight better than most people."

"Maybe you do, but I'm not quite sure."

"It's sort of like the rat. Remember the rat story?"

"Yes, of course."

"It's sort of like the rat. You make your first move and you do O.K. It's easier in the beginning. But, then they pitch you back up again, like the rat. You gotta let them pitch you up again if you stay in the game. They keep throwing you goddamn higher and higher till sooner or later you bust your ass."

The doctor leaned across his desk. "I see what you're saying, but some people make it. Right? Don't you know someone who has made it?"

"I know some people who are still *making it*. Not made it. They're still hanging on, getting slung up a little higher each time. But, they haven't *made it* yet."

"But, Billy, that's how life goes. Life is a series of challenges. We overcome them or we don't."

Billy took a paper clip from the desk and used the end to clean under his fingernails. He was silent for several seconds. "It ain't too fair, is it? You'd think they'd let you alone after a while."

The doctor was still tapping the side of his head. "Give me an example, Billy, of someone who should be left alone."

"Everyone."

"No, an example. Tell me about someone you know that gets thrown up again and again."

There were long moments of silence. "O.K.," the doctor continued, "what about someone who got thrown up that last time. You seem to feel very strongly about this."

"Yeah, sure, my old man. How's that? I know how you guys like this father-son crap. My old man."

"Tell me about him."

Billy cleared his throat. He tensed his leg muscles to walk back to the window, then relaxed. "The guy had it all, least by most people's standards. Was liked by everyone, had a good job. Was even a war hero. How about that? A through-and-through white-hat type of fellow. The kind that's supposed to win."

"And he didn't?"

"Some people would call it winning. He did O.K. for a guy off the block. But every time they threw him up, he came down just a little bit prouder. A little prouder each time. Things got to the point where if he wasn't working like hell to make sure he came down all right, he was lost. The man couldn't relax. Working, planning, figuring—it was always what we were going to do next year or the year after. Always something later."

Billy arched the paper clip towards a wastebasket. The clip bounced off the wall into the can. When he swallowed, the sound was loud. "But, I was proud of him. Goddamn, I was. I used to look at that medal of his and think about how I was going to be just like him. The guy was a winner; everyone said so. He was supposed to win."

Billy carefully rolled back the sleeves of his shirt. "I never realized how much a loser he was till I saw him lying there in his casket. It's funny, Doc, but he looked the very same. Didn't look dead or unnatural to me. People always say that, you know, how dead people look like they're made of wax. He looked the same. I realized then how little I had known him. My own dad didn't even look dead."

Billy rose this time and walked to the window. It was easier to talk from there. "I just wish someone had told him earlier he was doing things all wrong. That someone had gotten through to him and made him realize he didn't have to make it to the top of the hill. Not the very top. If they had just told him he didn't have to keep on being a hero. That no matter how high he went there was going to always be someone over him. Maybe things would have been different then. Maybe he would have looked dead to me there in his coffin."

Billy shut his eyes against the grayness beyond the window. He wished he could sling the loud clock through the glass.

"And you couldn't get through to him in time, Billy," the doctor said. "Isn't that what's eating at you?"

Billy whirled, framed black against the window. The outside light framed his hair like a halo. "You keep wanting to know why I cut people, Doc. Maybe it's like this. There's all those heroes out there. Brave men and heroes. Think they're gods or something. But, gods don't bleed, see. When I cut those guys, they bleed bad. Maybe they'll wise up then, realize they're no fucking god and are gonna have to find a way to live as men. Maybe I'm a martyr, Doc. Ever look at it that way? Maybe I'm really saving their lives." Billy bowed out his chest against the doctor's hard stare, but inside he felt very small.

WHEN Ruby heard from the short-order cook that Billy was going to fight, her first impulse was to wish that she hadn't given up the church. It was hard for her to feel her new prayers were rising above the grease smoke and clanging pots. Still, she prayed, while serving gobs of mashed potatoes, balancing hot plates on her arm, her words continuous behind pursed lips.

Many years had passed since Ruby attended the Methodist church off Grove Street. For several years after Larry's death, the church had been her only rationale for the world, her desperate belief that there must be someone who knew more than she, saw more, who understood why—when all she wanted out of life was to love and be loved—she had been denied all.

For five years after Larry died, Ruby thought often of killing herself. The night after his funeral, she had stood alone on the bank of the river, thinking how soothing the gray water looked, almost like a blanket she could slip under, never to hurt again. Her toes were almost in the water when she heard the faraway chimes of the church and stopped to listen, the sound strangely lilting on such a black day. Ruby turned and walked straight to the church, entered the unlocked door and walked to the altar. She intended to curse God but found herself unable to speak. She felt like she did when she wanted to fuss at Larry or Bubble, but her wrath changed to pity instead. Maybe God knew no more what he was doing than most men, she had thought. She sank to her knees, her prayer halfway between pleading and scolding.

Ruby existed but didn't live, ate but tasted nothing and saw the seasons pass in one long, dismal winter. Only on the church's carpeted floor with her face pressed in her hands could she see colors, Larry's face so bright as he sat eating supper and praising her, the way her children would have looked, her boys, little Rose in a brightly colored frock.

Ruby had nothing then but the church, her Sunday school class, Wednesday night prayer meeting. Mike was on his way up and blinded to anything not in his ultimate plan, and Bubble was already on his way down. But the church kept her going, kept her living if only in body, and set a cadence to the days that otherwise passed in a blur. The birth of Billy began to bring her back.

Ruby never had much use for the woman Mike married. She just had too much of all Ruby wished for herself. She was pretty and gay and slender and raven-haired and laughed so often, something Ruby had forgotten how to do. She wore new dresses that showed off her firm, round hips, and bright red lipstick, and took everything for granted. Mike was devoted to her, and if not particularly demonstrative, at least he was home every night. It was clear to Ruby that Bubble adored her. Ruby was incapable of being mean, accepted the young woman in time and, though never actually friends, loved her as family.

Billy was born in the third year of their marriage, a big-boned child with thick black hair. He came into the world screaming, and was placed atop his mother's breast to feed. Mollie was so frail, an uptown girl, fragile as a crystal vase, and not strong enough to give life and survive that gift. A week later she died.

Ruby's first sight of the child revealed to her that she still had a heart. It was like listening to a robin in the branches of a barren oak, one clear note building into a song. In the boy's wrinkled, red face she saw a reflection of what might have been and a glimpse of what still might be. From that second forth she loved him, loved him mightily as the weeks passed, loved him with the combined power she would have spent on Larry and the boys and little Rose.

Ruby was always thankful Mike wasn't a drinker, for he would have drunk himself to death that next year. Instead, he worked like one possessed, pulling overtime when he could, cutting firewood on his days off, anything that took him away from his house, where every corner still reeked of Mollie.

Ruby changed to the night shift and kept young Billy during the day, bathed him and changed him and cooed him to sleep, saw him first sit up and his first steps and heard him utter his first words. She stayed so busy, she didn't notice the darkness lifting from her heart.

Ruby took her first lover that summer, a trucker who drove out of Mississippi, tall and raw-boned, and though he was with her only a week, she shed warm tears at the end. If the boy could survive out of death and darkness, so could she; she would climb out of that dark pit and re-enter the world.

But she lost the church. At first, she tried reasoning through her prayers that giving love was far better than harboring desolation, but in the end, her guilt made her leave.

Now the cook had told her about Billy's fight. How nice it

would be to allow another to be strong for her. Shutting the storeroom door, she knelt, rested her head against a case of butter beans, and prayed.

The patrons of the east-side bars argued and debated and finally agreed that the best place for the fight was the parking lot behind the Cash-Way supermarket. The lot was off the usual beat of patroling policemen, and was close to the river in case flight became necessary. The lot was also large enough to provide plenty of fighting room, as well as for an eager crowd.

Billy was swept forward like a leaf carried down current on the river. The plans were no longer his, the fight wasn't his, it was just something he had to do. Fate's a bitch, he often thought.

"You'll whip him, buddy-roll," he heard as someone placed a beer in his hand. "Son of a bitch's gonna wish he never put his foot east of the river."

"Hey, man, we're all behind you," he heard from street corners. "He can't hang with a Riley."

"You ought to stop on by sometime," women told him. "I'd be good for your health."

Everyone had an expert strategy. "Kick him in the balls first, see? Then you can work on the side of his head like you please."

"Hell, no. Just shoot the motherfucker right in the beginning and don't worry about skinning up your knuckles."

"You'll take him anyway, Billy," everyone promised. "Can't no Yankee hang with someone from the east side."

Billy heard it all, saw the gleam in their eyes when they spoke of the fight, felt their slaps on his back while drinking their beer, and told himself over and over it was something he had to do.

"It's for us," their bright eyes screamed at him, the wallowing gray houses shouted, the hopelessness of the east side demanded. "We can't do it, but you can; you're Mike's son, and he could do it, and now it's passed on to you. Can't no man walk away from an ass whupping and still be a man, can't take an ass whupping lying down, gotta give it back to him, blow for blow, cut for cut—can't you still feel that blade in your back?—slice up his face and then we will all know you're the son of Mike, a Riley born here under the shadow of the mill, probably to die under that shadow, but proud, knowing you took it all and were still standing in the end."

BUBBLE was arrested midweek for stealing two bottles of rubbing alcohol from a Revco. Billy was called at work to come to the police station and bail him out. When he arrived, Bubble was sleeping in the drunk tank.

"Stock boy caught him going out the door with two bottles under his coat," the officer said. "When we got there, he was so drunk he couldn't stand."

Billy entered the cell to wake Bubble. His clothes were filthy and he reeked of wine and old sweat. His twitch had gotten worse, causing his left shoulder to jerk spasmodically. Billy wished he could close his eyes and not have to look. Finally, he bent and shook Bubble's arm. He moved and mumbled, but didn't awaken.

"We're not going to charge him," the policeman said. "Not this time. But you better get him in a hospital or something. When they get as bad as he is, they don't last long."

"We're trying to get him committed now," Billy said. "Soon as the papers clear the court, we're going to dry him out in the VA."

Billy had to wash Bubble's face with a wet rag before he came around. He sat up, belched and rubbed his eyes.

"Come on, Bubble," Billy said gently. "I'm going to take you home."

Bubble squinted his eyes, trying to focus. He pushed Billy's hand off his shoulder. "I ain't going nowhere with you. You're crazier than hell."

"Come on, Bubble," he said again. "Let's get a taxi and go over to Ruby's and get something to eat."

Bubble drew back. Ain't going with no crazy person. Mean

crazy. Always wanting to cut someone. Ya used to be a good boy. Mean crazy now."

Billy looked at the policeman, who frowned and shrugged. "Come on, Bubble." His voice cracked. "We gotta get you some help."

Bubble backed to the far side of the cell. "You wanna help me? Go buy me a jug. I'm dying for ya, hear? Get me a jug."

"You dying ain't going to help me, Bubble."

"Something's gotta help you. Gonna fight again. You've gone goddamn crazy."

Billy had to call Wallace to come before Bubble would leave. During the drive to Ruby's house, Bubble kept on about dying for Billy.

HAROLD had lasted longer than the others. For two months, he had stopped by on his trips up and down I-95. He never stayed longer than one night at a time, was often late and sometimes didn't come at all, but still he returned. He wasn't handsome, had a sharp nose and thinning, black hair and ears like curled cabbage leaves. He wasn't particularly intelligent, either, had quit school in the eighth grade and had difficulty reading even newspapers, his love life no more fortunate, having married twice, both times for less than a year. But regardless of all his faults, he was kind and gentle and devoted to Ruby. He brought her flowers and dime-store perfume, took her to movies, but was also content when sitting beside her watching television. Many people wouldn't have considered him a prize, but he kept coming back, something no other man had done.

Ruby was sitting at the table reading from her King James Bible when someone knocked.

"What are you doing here?" she said, opening the door. "I didn't expect you tonight."

Harold stepped inside, kissed Ruby's cheek and handed her a dozen red roses. "I got a load going down to Tampa. Just left

Richmond a few hours ago. Can't stay but an hour or so."

"And you stopped by here? You shouldn't a' made a trip out of the way. And roses. You ought not to be spending your money on me." Ruby pulled him against her breast.

"I ought to bring you more than flowers. Woman as fine as you."

Ruby stuck the roses in a large mason jar and filled it with water. Then she hurried to put on a pot of coffee. "You're gonna have to drive all night now. You're gonna need lots of coffee."

Harold picked up her Bible from the table. "Been reading the Good Book, I see. Have I drove you to religion?"

"Lord, honey, I just wish everyone was as sweet as you. Sometimes, I feel that between Billy and Bubble, I'll pull every hair out of my head."

"Don't you touch a hair on that pretty head of yours."

"Bubble's drinking himself to death somewhere right this second, and Billy. I'm not even going to worry about Billy tonight."

Harold turned on the television and lowered himself to the couch. Ruby brought over two cups of coffee. He crossed his legs, then uncrossed them and blew wrinkles in his coffee. He cleared his throat.

"Honey, you're nervous as a cat," Ruby said.

Harold stood and walked to a ceramic punch bowl Ruby displayed on an end table. He picked up the ladle.

"I'm nervous 'cause I got something on my mind," Harold finally said. "Something that concerns me and you."

Ruby felt her heart begin to pound. Here it comes, she thought. Just when I was beginning to hope he might be the one. "Well," she began, "for heavens sake, just say what's on your mind."

Harold set his cup on the edge of the end table. "There's this job opening, see. With Green Lines, operating out of Fayetteville. I think I can get it."

Ruby felt her heart take an even bigger leap. She clamped her jaws to keep from shrieking.

"I think I got a real good chance of getting it," he continued. "Me and the dock manager go back a ways. What would you think about me being around here more often?" His words were slow, thick, and he often stopped to lick his lips. "You're liable to get tired of me."

"You talk plum silly. Of course I wouldn't get tired of you. Why, it would tickle me to death to see you more than once a week."

Harold returned to the couch. "I'd like it. Like it a lot." He cleared his throat again. "I been thinking, Ruby. I know we only been going together a little over two months now. I know that ain't long, but I've sure come to think something of you."

Ruby took his hand and squeezed it.

"I was just thinking," he continued, "that maybe after a while longer, so we'll know each other better and all, that if you want to, I know I ain't got a lot to offer you, but maybe we might get married. That is, if you'd have me?"

Ruby's throat suddenly ached, and though she blinked hard, tears spilled down her face. Harold reached and hugged her while she sobbed.

"I'm sorry," she said, rubbing her eyes. "Blubbering like a young'un. I'd be proud to be your wife some day, Harold. Mighty proud."

Harold waited until she was smiling again before he removed his arms from her neck. He slumped against the back of the couch, lit a cigarette and smoked in silence for a minute. "I got a little problem, Ruby. And I don't know what to do about it."

"Well, what's the matter?" she asked, light from the lamp splintering into colors through her tears. "It can't be something we can't handle together."

Harold studied his feet stacked on the coffee table. "It's the credit union at Roadway. I owe them some money still. I got to pay it off before I can leave, so they'll give me a decent recommendation."

"Is that all?" Ruby asked. "That ain't no problem, honey."

"I don't have it, Ruby. I don't have near that much."

"How much you owe?"

"Almost two thousand dollars. I had to buy some new tires a while back."

Ruby chewed her lip as she thought. "I have it, honey. I have a little money saved that I can loan you."

He stared into Ruby's shiny eyes. "I hate to ask, baby. God knows I do."

"Hush," she said and leaned to hug him. "You just hush right now. I don't mind one bit."

"I appreciate it, baby. And, I'll pay you back quick. Soon as I get settled in." He counted on his fingers. "Finish in Tampa tomorrow. Get back to Richmond by Wednesday and settle up. Shoot, no later than Friday night, I'll come rolling in here free as a bird."

Ruby fumbled through her purse for her checkbook. Her hands trembled. Every atom of common sense she possessed told her to stop, not to hand her life savings away to a man who might never come back. But this one time, she kept telling herself, this one time maybe she would be right. She clutched the Bic so hard her knuckles turned white.

BUBBLE returned to the wino camp behind Willie's. Billy and Ruby tried to persuade him to come live at Ruby's, but he only cussed as he continued to pack a small suitcase. There was no way they could stop him until the commitment papers came through, and Wallace said that would take some time. Bubble sold his few remaining tools, junked his old car, and stalked away from the house he had rented for nineteen years.

A storeroom opened to the back lot of Willie's. The window had been busted out years before, and the door slid on one hinge, but the room was dry and out of the wind, and as long as the winos bought steadily and didn't fight, Willie opened it for them in winter. The bums covered the floor with newspaper, nailed cardboard over the window, and kept reasonably warm from the glow of a coal fire.

Bubble took his place along the wall, between Shorty and Jimbo. Chubby had a pocket of money from picking apples in Asheville and was therefore now sleeping with Wilma.

"You're quite a slut," Bubble told her as he folded cardboard to make a bed. "Quite a slut."

"You're quite a goddamn drunk, too," she said. "We had it good, and you had to drink it all away."

"Quite a double-crossing slut."

"She ain't no slut," Chubby said. "I don't like you calling my ole lady a slut."

"You're a bigger slut than she is," Bubble answered. "Hey, you got a jug?"

"I told you, Bubble, you better slow down," Shorty said. "You're looking worse every day."

"Looking better, feeling better," Bubble said. "What you say, Chubby? Gonna give me a drink?"

Chubby swore softly as he reached into his coat. He pulled out a pint of Thunderbird, took a swallow, and passed it to Bubble. Bubble turned up the bottle and chugged. Shorty watched, slowly shaking his head.

RUBY worked the night shift on Friday until midnight and watched the lights of every truck that entered the parking lot, but never saw Harold's silver-cabbed Peterbilt. She even took thirty minutes longer than usual cleaning up her section, craning her neck around at the sound of every semi gearing down, but no Harold.

"I didn't have any phone calls you didn't tell me about, did I, Joe?" Ruby asked the cook.

He shook his head. "Ruby, you know I'd have hollered for you."

She slowly drove to the east side, crossed the bridge pretending to look at the water and telling herself it didn't matter if she didn't see the taillights of his trailer parked in front of her house. Inside the house, she straightened up for awhile, then put on a pot of coffee and lay down to watch Johnny Carson. Once the phone rang and she hurried for it, heart pounding. It was a wrong number. Finally, she fell asleep on the couch.

17

SATURDAY came gray and cold with a heavy wet wind out of the east. Billy lay in bed long after he had awakened, staring at drops of moisture clinging to the window screen, and beyond to the wet-shiny branches.

He felt strong now, his arm was fully mended and the cuts crossing his back were only jagged pink scars, still tender when he rolled his shoulders against the sheets.

Before going to sleep the night before, he had wondered if he would dream of the coming fight. It bothered him that he might dream of losing, so he tried an old childhood trick. Billy closed his eyes and thought hard of the fight, imagined getting cut in his belly and then shot. The trick had worked when he was a kid for warding off dreams of monsters, and it worked again. He slept straight through the night.

Billy wasn't ashamed that he hoped the soldier wouldn't show. He wasn't afraid, but he wasn't stupid. No, damn it, I am afraid, he thought. Man starts not being afraid, something's wrong with his head. Maybe he's more afraid than me?

The fight was scheduled for eight that night. Word was leaked to the police that the men would meet at midnight. Long before they discovered the truth, it would be settled, one on one, as simple as that. No cops, no charges, just two men with a bad thing between them.

Billy rolled to the edge of the bed and sat up. The tiled floor was cold, so he pulled on his socks before walking into the kitchen. He took a quart jar filled with lime Kool-Aid out of the refrigerator and poured a glass. He took a doughnut from a box on the counter. Hell of a breakfast, he thought, for a man fighting for his ass tonight. He turned on the television to reruns of the Three Stooges and settled down in an old rocking chair. Their violence did not seem as funny as usual, and he soon turned the channel. From the window, he watched people passing below. Very few were out on such a miserable morning.

Billy had been trying hard lately to hate the soldier. After all, it was he who had cut and shamed him on his own turf, and was still pushing the fight. Billy made himself think of how bad his back had burned as the blade sliced through his skin, how pebbles had embedded deep in his knees. He tried to hate the soldier, but all he felt was an emptiness as gray as the morning.

Guess it's just that way, he thought, there are some things a person has to do and not ask why.

Billy left the apartment at midday, keeping to side streets to avoid people. He wore an old military raincoat turned up at the collar. He wove a path through back alleys and yards till he reached the riverbank. The bank was slick and muddy, but he scrambled through the brush to the overgrown fishing trail running along shore. Water from an earlier rain dripped from the branches and beaded on his coat. Billy started downriver, away from the roar of tires on the bridge. He walked nearly a half mile, till he was at the old barge wreck. It lay partly on its side, half on shore. A sandbar had formed on its ebb side. Billy climbed into the rusty skeleton and sat under a panel of sheet metal where the sand was dry. From there, he could see up and down the river.

In earlier times, he and Bubble had come here occasionally to fish off the barge for large catfish that lurked in its shade. The barge had once carried coal from the port at Wilmington, but as a child, Billy had often imagined the wreck as the remains of a pirate's schooner. He knew from history that Blackbeard had once frequented the mouth of the river.

The current was strong from the night's rain, the water

muddy and littered with branches and half submerged logs. The debris swiftly floated past, only yards beyond the barge blending into obscurity against the river.

Wish I could just lay down in the water, Billy thought, and let it carry me. See just where I end up. Let it carry me away.

Though Billy had always enjoyed being on the river, he had always found it a bit frightening too, his inability to ever see more than a few hundred yards in either direction. On occasion, he had imagined the river as being only one short length that flowed eternally out of oblivion and into it. He never knew what was coming next from around the far bend, or where it would disappear to afterwards. The current passed, carrying its refuse quietly and unceasingly.

Rain began to fall again, a soundless drizzle on the steel hull. Billy watched moisture pool in a crease in the metal. The moisture ran down the crease to the edge of the sheet metal, consolidating into a silver teardrop, clinging above the dark river. The drop grew heavier from runoff and trembled on the edge, its colors clear and sparkling even in the poor light. Finally, it fell, splatted into the water and disappeared instantly. Billy felt a shiver run across his shoulders. He climbed back through the brown, barren ribs and started through the rain for town.

Ruby, working the day shift, concerned herself with small tasks usually done at closing: filling the salt shakers and sugar bowls, emptying ash trays, wiping the windows and occasionally lifting prayers skyward through the grease smoke. She refused to let herself search any longer for the glint of Harold's chromed cab, and she tried hard not to think too often of Billy. She just worked with an intensity that made the other waitresses keep out of her way and the truckers keep their wisecracks to themselves. When Billy appeared at the door, she sloshed tea on the tray she was carrying.

"What you doing out in this kind of weather? You're going to be sick as a dog." She hurried over with a cup and coffeepot, trying to hold her hand steady while she poured. "This is terrible weather to be out in."

"I was just walking around some and thought I'd stop in."

"Well, you have to eat something. I bet you haven't had a mouthful all day."

"I'm not hungry, Ruby. You're all the time trying to feed me."

"Well, it's 'cause I love you, honey. Men never do look after themselves half right."

"I'm a big boy, Ruby. A grown man."

Ruby's lip quivered, and she sat heavily in the booth. She stopped pretending. "You're not really going to fight that man, are you Billy? You're not really going to do it?"

Billy slowly stirred sugar into his coffee.

"Is that why you came by here? To tell me you won't fight?" Ruby stopped and rubbed her face. "I've been making myself stay out of this, son. Wallace said I should and I realize you're a grown man and don't want some old fat woman telling you how to act. But, Billy, have you *thought* about what happened last time? That man might—he might . . ."

Billy put his hand up. "Calm down. You're going to give yourself a heart attack."

"But, you don't even seem worried." Ruby wrung her hands. "Haven't you even thought about what can happen?"

"I'm not fighting him, Ruby."

Ruby's eyes widened and she reached across the table to grab his arm. "Do you mean that, Billy? You mean it?"

"I mean it, Ruby. Stop worrying so much."

"You look me in the eye and say that." Ruby gripped his arm tighter. "Come on. Look me in the eye and promise you're not going to fight."

Billy lifted his eyes for a moment. "I promise. See there."

Ruby knew Billy's eyes like no two others in the world, and she knew he was lying. Or if not lying, at least he was undecided. Her chest ached, knowing he had come by so she wouldn't worry. Ruby released his arm but stayed hunched over the table. "I want you to listen to me, Billy. I ain't gonna make no scene. I'm just gonna tell you I love you, and I have faith in you. O.K?"

Billy downed the last of his coffee and stood. "I'll see you later, Ruby." He bent quickly and pecked her on one cheek, then strode out the door.

Ruby watched him go. She heard the hiss of brakes from another semi, but didn't look. But she would wait. She would wait on Billy and Harold and Bubble. Even if she had to wait the rest of her life, she would, and would continue to hope. Without hope, there was nothing.

BUBBLE stayed passed out until late Saturday morning. The night before he had drunk Mad Dog until he puked, then drunk some more. Now, the other winos watched him twitch and mumble in his sleep.

Bubble woke with a start, rolled onto his back and sat up. The pain in his belly made him grit his teeth. He pushed his fist against his gut and held it there. His twitch was now so bad that whenever he relaxed his shoulder it jerked. He tried to spit but the thick saliva stuck to his tongue.

Wilma brought him a cup of chicken and rice soup. She knelt beside him and touched his arm. "Drink this, Bubble. You got to eat something."

Bubble pushed the cup from in front of his face. "I don't want nothing."

"You got to eat, Bubble. If you don't you're gonna be real sick."

"Get da hell out of my face."

Wilma raised the cup to Bubble's lips and held it there until he took a swallow. At first he gagged, but then drank till the cup was empty. Wilma moved back to the warmth of the fire. Bubble wiped sleep from the corners of his eyes.

"Hey, Bubble," Shorty called. "You want some of these beans?

I got plenty here." Shorty was bent over an old coffee can he was using as a pot. He stirred the beans with a skinned stick.

"Don't want no beans," Bubble mumbled. "I need a drink worse."

"No, you don't need a drink," Shorty answered. "That's the last thing you need."

"I need a goddamn drink bad."

"You need beans." Shorty left his cooking to stand over Bubble. "You need a doctor, too, son. You're looking mighty bad."

"Fuck a doctor; ain't nothing a drink won't cure. Shorty, how 'bout getting me something to drink."

Shorty shook his head. "You need beans and a doctor. I'll tote you on my back if you'll go to the doctor, but I ain't gonna buy you no wine."

Bubble tried to spit again. "Fuck it." He reached into his pocket and pulled out some bills. "Hey, Jimbo," he shouted across the room. "You fly and I buy?"

Jim hungrily licked his lips at the money, but Shorty stared at him and shook his head. Jimbo looked at the ground.

"Well, fuck da whole goddamn lot of you. I'll just get it myself."

It took several minutes for him to get to his feet and weave to the door. He held to the doorframe and cradled his belly, then disappeared outside.

"They gonna commit him," Wilma whispered when Bubble had gone. "I went to tell Ruby how bad he is, and she said they were just waiting for the papers next week."

"Next week is a long time," Shorty said. "A long, long time for him."

Bubble was half through his first bottle before the burning in his gut and his twitching eased. He moved closer to the fire to warm his feet. As drunkenness washed over him, he relented and passed the bottle.

"You always were a mighty kind fellow," Shorty said. "That's why I hate to see you drinking so bad."

"I'm doing it for Billy."

"You right sure, Bubble, you ain't just using him as an excuse."

"I hear he's gonna fight tonight," Chubby said across the fire. "I heard he's gonna fight that soldier who cut him up."

"Ain't gonna be no fight," Bubble said.

"That's the talk. Everybody's talking 'bout it."

"Naw, he won't fight. You just wait and see."

By late afternoon, Bubble was ripped again, singing and shouting drunk, perched against the wall with a bottle jammed between his knees. Mike's face flared in the fire, growing until it filled most of the room.

"No, goddamn it," Bubble shouted, "don't come in here fucking with me now, cause I'm dying for the boy."

Mike blinked and shimmered, his face red like the flames. A sneer covered his fiery mouth. "You're dying all right. Soon, too. But, it ain't for Billy."

"Dying good for 'im, hear me, big brother."

The other winos fell silent and watched Bubble talk into the air. Wilma turned her face.

"Yep, dying damn good for the boy, cause I love him." Bubble took a long guzzle of wine, the liquid spilling from the corners of his mouth. "Wanna tell you something else there, Brother." Bubble spit some wine towards Mike. "Reckon I ought to tell you, since we're soon to be equals. I loved his mama, too. I can say it now. Hear that, Mike? I loved his mama."

Mike's face splintered into swirling colors, then reappeared. "You think I didn't know you loved her? It was written all over your face. But, that's all right, Bubble. I had her."

"Wouldn't a' much longer. We were going away. Me and her and Billy."

Mike laughed. "But, you didn't. Like all the other things you never did."

Mike splintered into colors again, but this time disappeared. Bubble stared into the gloom. "Goddamn told him, didn't I."

Bubble scowled at the winos watching. "What the hell ya'll staring at," he yelled. "I was talking to my brother. Told him a thing or two; told him I loved his wife. Told him a thing or two."

Bubble cocked his head when he first heard the sound, a far off noise almost like scratching a wall. It gradually grew in volume like far-off thunder. "Ya'll hear that?" Bubble asked. He cupped his hand behind one ear.

"I don't hear nothing," Shorty said.

"No, listen. Sound like something rumbling."

Bubble leaned forward and listened, his face hard, one eye squinted. "Sounds like the ocean, sort of."

Bubble imagined a swarm of worms sweeping through the door, thousands of them, shaggy and green with glowing red eyes. They spread across the floor like a flood, over the empty bottles and piles of trash. Bubble's jaw dropped in horror and a scream began deep in his throat. He slung his bottle at the advancing swarm, but it only shattered against the wall, the worms leaving slime on the shards. He backed against the wall until the worms reached his feet and began to climb his trousers. He stomped and swatted them, but for every one he knocked away, a hundred took its place. As he writhed, Bubble screamed for help.

"Poor bastard," Shorty muttered while Bubble tried to climb the wall. "Poor damn bastard."

Bubble flung out his arms, staring at the worms that covered them. The worms began to burrow under his skin. "Oh, God, help me," he screamed. "Shorty, they're eating me alive."

"Take it easy, son. We'll get you to the hospital." Shorty took a couple of cautious steps towards Bubble. "Call an ambulance," he said over his shoulder. "Easy, Bubble. I'll get them off ya."

Bubble cowered against the wall, his eyes glazed. Without warning, he charged the door, knocking down Shorty. For several minutes they listened to his shouts grow dimmer as he disappeared into the brush beside the river.

18

A CROWD began to gather in the deserted parking lot at seven o'clock. All the local bad boys were there; the Johnsons, the Bains, the mob of Lynch brothers, Jerry from the drive-in, plus an assortment of east siders, men in painters' pants, mill uniforms, Terry Autry straight from the fish market with scales stuck to his clothes. There were plenty of women, too: Marge Thompson and her sister, Connie, the Hawley sisters, Patty Boyd and a carload of Lumbee Indian gals who had driven up from Raeford, all in tight shirts and jeans, reeking of perfume.

A mist was still falling, but the sky had lightened just before sunset and the mood of everyone was high as a carnival. Tony had closed his bar and was selling cold beer from the boot of his car, and there were plenty of loose joints for sale. Someone had lit a grill and was selling hotdogs. A sentry watched for police cars, but since it wasn't illegal to watch a fight, there was little to fear except for those holding pot. The beer and whiskey went down quickly between bursts of rapid, excited talk.

A few minutes before eight, the jacked-up Chevy came whumping into the parking lot, its lights cut off. The driver circled the lot a couple of times before shutting down facing the street. The sun-shade soldier got slowly out of the car, peering cautiously over the lenses at the group silently watching him. He was followed by four other short-haired men wearing heavy coats, at least one hand in their pockets. They kept their backs to the car.

"Where's your boy?" the soldier asked. "He chicken out?"

"You won't be calling him 'boy' after tonight's over," one of the Johnsons said. "You'll be calling him 'mister.' "

"I'll be calling him dead boy. Deader-than-hell boy." The man leaned against his car, picking his nails with a matchstick.

"I wouldn't be too goddamn sure," another said.

Billy had been sitting on the roof for more than an hour, watching the people from underneath a poncho. He could look over the skyline of the east side, yellow and fuzzy through the mist. He watched them all come, heard their laughter and curses, the "ka-chunk" of opened beers, saw the glow of passed joints, sharp shadows cast by the parking lot flood lamp. He watched the Chevy turn in, heard its cammed engine and heard the soldier call him boy.

Billy felt as if he had an immortal power over those below, as if he was watching a play that could only continue when he, the main character, entered. He glanced at his watch. Three minutes to eight.

Billy felt his back pocket, where the handle of his knife bulged solidly against the fabric. He knew Tony was holding a sawed-off cue stick, and if needed, a military forty-five.

Three fucking minutes, Billy thought. One hundred eighty seconds and I'm going to fight this guy and one of us is going to get hurt bad. He hated the crowd of on-lookers, so smug and expectant. What did they have to lose, anyway?

"Your boy don't show up by five past, I'm leaving," the soldier said. "I got better things to do than wait around for some punk."

"You'll be wishing he never showed up," Tony shouted. "You'll be wishing to hell you never drove over that river the first time."

Several people laughed and cracked new beers. The soldier spit on the ground. Billy watched.

To fight was easier. Billy knew he was good at fighting. He was expected to fight. But to walk away?

The soldier's voice rose again. "Looks like you bad boy ain't gonna show." He again looked at his watch. "Looks to me like he might just be chicken shit."

"You just hold on," the people of the east side shouted, "and you'll see who's chicken shit. Billy Riley ain't scared of nothing."

The soldier held his watch up again. Billy grinned. Asshole seems in a hurry to leave, he thought.

"Yeah, you just give him thirty more seconds," Tony said. "He'll show. Billy's our man. Our main man."

At that moment the decision was made for Billy—not monumental nor epic, but easily. *Our* man. *Our* Billy. *Our* warrior. *Our* puppet. He understood how much their man he had been for the past months. Mike's son was their man.

He thought again of Cassie and the acorns. Maybe she had it right, that we weren't all intended to make it, but there was a plan, a system behind the seemingly chaotic fate. Maybe the struggles of one did boost the efforts of the next? But, one thing she did have wrong, he was certain—we must continue to love and to hope—together.

A cry started deep in his gut and swept before it the darkness he had harbored since his father's death. His bellow drowned out all other sounds, echoed off the distant factory walls and rolled over him again. The crowd below searched the sky for its maker, silent, startled eyes peering into the night.

Billy quickly crossed the flat roof to the drainpipe. He left his rage then, gripped the pipe and swung down into the street and faded into the night. He knew he had to find Bubble fast, to tell him what he had learned. Only Billy could save himself.

BILLY jogged through the glistening streets toward Willie's. He swung the door wide and stepped into the smoky, dim room.

"Where's Bubble?" he shouted to the gray shapes huddled around the fire. "Hey, Bubble! You in here?"

There was silence. Wilma moved from the ring of light.
"Hey, Wilma. You seen Bubble tonight?"
She shuffled closer. "He's bad off, Billy." Wilma hunched her shoulders as if afraid of being hit. "Bubble's bad sick."
"Where is he? He in the hospital?"
Wilma huddled lower. No. He's down by the boat landing. We tried to get him back here Billy, but he wouldn't come."
"What's the matter with him?"
"Just bad sick. Bad sick. Seeing things and hollering and all."

BILLY found him lying in the weeds beside the steep river bank. He was face down in the mud with his knees drawn close to his belly. Rain had soaked his clothes, and he was shivering uncontrollably. The twitch in his left side had become violent, jerking his body with contractions. A puddle of his vomit was dark red with blood. Billy knelt and gently shook his shoulder. Bubble moaned but didn't wake.
"Poor old fellow," Billy whispered. The joy left him like a candle flame on the wind. "Poor old dumb Bubble."
But he had been expecting this. It was as if Bubble had been dead for months, as if his spirit had left weeks earlier. Behind was this casing of a man, a shell of comical, generous Bubble. The form shivering in the mud was like the shed skin of a snake, the exact replica of how its wearer had looked, but as lifeless as a fallen leaf.
Billy lifted Bubble's head from the mud and laid his own folded jacket beneath. He saw the gray skin, half-open eyes, and the yellow crud in their corners. He watched Bubble's labored breathing, saw his back rise and fall and heard the air whistle through his nose. He continued to jerk, and with each spasm slid a couple more inches down the incline, closer to the drop.
Ain't no use in going for help, Billy thought. Bubble's been dead for weeks now. Billy made his second big decision of the night: he waited.

"Thanks old man," Billy said. "You did save me. You sure did."

As Billy sat there, he remembered the good times he and Bubble had spent together.

"You remember them all, Bubble? You remember all those times? How about that tree fort we built in the chinaberry tree? Remember how it had a trap door on the bottom, and there was a rope ladder that could be pulled up? Remember that time when I was little and ran away, and Ruby and Dad were searching for me down by the river. You circled back straight to the fort, and we sat there for a couple of hours eating the peanut-butter sandwiches I had brought and talking. And how about the time you took me to see *Toby Tyler,* and I got to crying afterwards because I wanted a trunk like the elephant, and you made me one out of a sock filled with sand. And the telescope. God. How many hours you think we spent shivering at night in the back yard, looking up in the sky and trying to read astronomy books with a flashlight? I'll never forget those nights."

The minutes passed while Bubble jerked closer to the drop-off. Billy continued to talk.

"And the county fair. We went together nearly every year. At first, I was scared to ride anything that left the ground, but you would coax me to try it, and after a couple of years there wasn't a thing there I wouldn't ride. And that time when I was twelve, and you slipped me into the hoochie-coochie, and then later while we were eating corn dogs, answered all my questions about how babies come. And the river, Bubble. I wouldn't trade a million dollars for those times. They were the best. Remember when we'd camp on a sandbar and fish all night, frying up big pans of bullhead fillets and hush puppies? Remember how good it smelled? And when I was older and we'd bring along a case of beer and let it cool in the river, and you'd tell me stories about Mama. The shad would be running, and we'd go down below the lock. Here would come a big run and the water would be churning around the boat, and you'd be gaffing them with a hook and slinging them on board. I'd get so excited I'd be shouting. How about it, Bubble? Weren't those the best times?"

The rain stopped. There came the first stirring of a breeze from the east. Billy talked and Bubble jerked and slid further till he hung on the edge of the bank.

"And when I was in boot camp, and you drove all the way down to Parris Island, and you got me out on visitor pass, and we drove to the picnic grounds beside the sound and ate cold fried chicken sitting in the sand."

Billy remembered and talked and wasn't sad, just sorry their good times had to end. He watched Bubble's gray face and recalled how it used to look, bright blue eyes and such a quick, broad smile. A break in the clouds appeared and Billy saw several dim stars.

"And I'll always know where to find Saturn." He pointed. "She's right over in that direction, shines sort of yellow. How many people can point out Saturn? Not very many."

With a final jerk, Bubble went over the edge of the bank. One shoulder dropped first; then his body rolled slowly, the way a large tree twists as it begins to fall. He turned on his side, his face appearing briefly in the dim light, then rolled to his back and began to slide down the hill. Billy watched him go, his movement graceful—dance-like in its slow motion. Down he slid, over mud and wet leaves, gathering speed and reaching the water in seconds.

"So long," Billy whispered, his breath catching in his chest.

The water splashed softly, covering Bubble except for his calves and feet. Ripples spread out from his body and lost themselves in the dark stretch of the river. Soon the water was smooth as glass, as restful as a lullabye.

A breeze stirred the branches and passed over Billy, softly, as if Bubble's soul was leaving the cold water. Billy waited and felt no shame at the tears that burned his cheeks. Later, he went to the pay phone in front of Willie's and called the rescue squad.

BILLY quietly turned the key, slowly opened the door and stepped inside. Midnight had passed, the parking lights were shut off and the store was dark. He closed the door and waited till he could see. Forms began slowly to appear, and there rose the sleepy mews and whimpers of the animals. Billy soothed them with his whispers. Their smell was warm and pungent. When he could see, he walked to the rats' cage and knelt at the wire. The rats were huddled in a bunch, but when Billy opened the door, they stirred, blinking and sniffing the air. A couple ambled over seeking food. Billy counted them.

He placed ten in a plastic wash pail, then carried the pail outside. He tipped it over the sidewalk till the rats slid out. They were frightened and huddled again on the cold concrete.

"Go on," Billy hissed. "Get the hell out of here."

He hurried back into the store to refill the bucket. As the cluster of rats grew larger, a few brave ones began to explore the edge of their circle. They sniffed the cold air and felt under their hairless feet the strange new texture of concrete. Billy made four trips before he emptied the cage.

"Go on, get," he said. "What in the world is wrong with you guys?"

He nudged one with his shoe, but the rat squealed and squatted. When a car passed, Billy lay flat on the sidewalk, but it drove out of sight.

One rat started the exodus. He broke from the circle, down the lip of the sidewalk onto the wet gravel. He waddled over the wet stones, his fat belly swaying. Another followed. Then two more separated from the group in another direction. Soon, all were departing, small white bodies quickly swallowed by the night. Billy watched until the last one disappeared.

Inside the store, he opened the cash register and placed a

handful of bills in the drawer. Then he locked the door as he left.

BILLY wandered the streets of Fayetteville filled with grief for Bubble. By the silent houses he walked, upon wet leaves carpeting the sidewalk, passing sleeping families, trash cans stacked by the curb, cats slinking between shadows. He walked slowly, trying not to think, instead concentrating on placing each foot carefully, feeling life radiate the length of his foot every time his heels struck pavement.

On the river bridge he stopped in the middle of the span, where he could see best into the bowels of the east side. He climbed over the railing and stood on the narrow lip of concrete where there was nothing between him and his view but the cold night air. Below was the sound of moving water, but he couldn't see the river, only a blackness beneath that whispered from the current. He stood waiting, tucked within night's dark blanket.

And with the dawn, the people of the east side began to awaken, one bedroom window shining clear in the black, then another and another. Billy knew each light so well—a woman stirring grits for her husband seated at the table, his head cradled in his hands, mill people pulling on overalls still stiff from yesterday's grime, table waiters and short-order cooks rising to prepare breakfast for those fortunate enough to sleep late, plumbers and carpenters sipping coffee before driving across the river to continue building those split-levels, the winos behind Willie's beginning to stir, tasting metal in their mouths as they wondered where that next bottle would come from. Working-class people, fighting people, hoping people, some day making-it people.

The eastern sky was flaming from the remnants of the past storm. A milk truck crossed the bridge and tooted as it passed, a single car, then the grumble of a silver-cabbed Peterbilt as it geared down coming home. A waning moon balanced the sunrise from the west, the oval huge and silver. Sea of Tranquility, Billy said softly, noting a dark impression in the orb. Turning back to the railing, he paused. They'll keep throwing you up, Billy boy, he thought. Higher and higher. He shrugged. Just let them try.